fresh catch

KATE CANTERBARY

VESPER PRESS

about fresh catch

Take a vacation, they said. *Get away from Silicon Valley's back-stabbing and power-grabbing. Recharge the innovative batteries. Unwind, then come back stronger than ever.*

Instead, I got lost at sea and fell in love with an anti-social lobsterman.

There's one small issue:
Owen Bartlett doesn't know who I am. Who I really am.

***

I don't like people.

I avoid small talk and socializing, and I kick my companions out of bed before the sun rises. No strings, no promises, no problems.

Until Cole McClish's boat drifts into Talbott's Cove, and I bend all my rules for the sexy sailor.

I don't know Cole's story or what he's running from, but one thing is certain:
I'm not letting him run away from me.

This is a work of fiction. Names, characters, places, and incidents are the product of the author's imagination or are used fictitiously, and any resemblance to actual persons, living or dead, business establishments, events, or locales is entirely coincidental.

Copyright © 2018 by Kate Canterbary

All rights reserved. No part of this book may be reproduced, stored in a retrieval system, or transmitted in any forms, or by any means, electronic, mechanical, photocopying, recording, or otherwise, without prior written permission of the author.

Trademarked names appear throughout this book. Rather than use a trademark symbol with every occurrence of a trademarked name, names are used in an editorial fashion, with no intention of infringement of the respective owner's trademark(s).

Editing provided by Julia Ganis of Julia Edits.

Proofreading provided by Marla Esposito of Proofing Style.

Cover design provided by Anna Crosswell of Cover Couture.

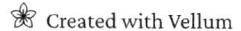

❦ Created with Vellum

preface

I want you to know
one thing

You know how this is:
if I look
at the crystal moon, at the red branch
of the slow autumn at my window,
if I touch
near the fire
the impalpable ash
or the wrinkled body of the log,
everything carries me to you,
as if everything that exists,
aromas, light, metals,
were little boats
that sail
toward those isles of yours that wait for me.

from "If You Forget Me" by Pablo Neruda

For Nick and Erin,
the ones who started it all.

one

COLE

Adrift: *adj. Floating without being either moored or steered.*

"OH, FOR FUCK'S SAKE!" I yelled, pounding my fist against the sonar system's housing. It was the only tool I knew to be functional, but now the screen was black. "Fuck, fuck, *fuck*."

This was bad. I was officially in the shit, and more shit than my usual.

Abandoning the boat's failing navigation system, I stormed into the captain's quarters for my laptop and tools. It was dark in there, darker than at the helm, and it heightened my senses. The summer air was thick and close, and sweat was rolling down my back. My belly was rumbling with hunger and my eyes were bleary from straining to spot rocks and land through the heavy veil of night.

I wanted air conditioning, whiskey, sushi, and a good night's sleep. In that order.

"Un-fucking-likely," I murmured as I returned to the boat's control center.

The screen indicated I was minutes away from reaching my destination at Newburyport Harbor, but the sea and shore were dark. Too dark to be anywhere near a port city.

If not for the lighthouse shining in the distance, I would think I was miles from shore.

"If this is what I get for investing in start-ups," I muttered, "then start-ups can go fuck themselves."

I snorted at that notion and set to unscrewing the control panel. If it weren't for start-up investors, I wouldn't have been the youngest billionaire in history. But founding an all-things-internet company and making it a household name wasn't as golden and glossy as the media made it seem.

According to the company's public statements, I was on sabbatical. It was a good cover story, and my spokeswoman managed to weave in some cozy anecdotes about my childhood love of sailing to make it feel even more authentic. It was handy that I did love sailing. Or, I *had* loved it, back when my summers were spent helping my uncle build custom boats in Morro Bay. But that was a lifetime ago.

The truth was that my board of directors had ejected me from the CEO's seat after my latest initiative fell below Silicon Valley's expectations. Project DaVinci was supposed to turn the industry upside down. Instead of doing that, it was a gigantic flop that yielded nothing worthy of my company's name.

All told, the billions spent on that endeavor were nowhere near as painful as the landslide of bad press.

This was the first time I'd *ever* taken a true vacation, one without a whiff of work, since founding the company in my apartment three blocks from Harvard University's Cambridge, Massachusetts campus. I wasn't one for lavish holidays or extreme adventures. I was like all the other Red Bull-addled programmers who found it easier to admire smartly constructed code than the natural world.

I hated this PR-inspired bullshit walkabout. If it wasn't for my desire to keep my stock prices from plummeting, I would've thrown a bigger fit when the board stripped me of my control and saddled me with a lame title. Chief Innovations Officer was a long, hard fall from CEO.

I was known for that—fit-throwing. I wasn't especially proud of it, and I'd worked my ass off to get my temper under control in the early years of my success, but it still followed me. Any glimmer of impatience was filed under my storied tyrannical management style known widely as Scream, Fire, and Throw. There had been tell-all books written by people who didn't care about violating nondisclosure agreements. The ass-lickers called it a new, disruptive style of leadership. The haters petitioned Amnesty International to add me to their watch lists.

Over the years, I'd changed. But that didn't rewrite my history. For an environment that evolved by the nanosecond, the half-life of bad behavior was eternity.

I'd matured from the slouchy geek who'd changed the way people spent their time on the internet. I was still arrogant and more condescending than necessary, but now

I kept all of that close to my bespoke vests. My chief of staff, Neera Malik, beat some corporate manners into me and helped me recognize the negative impact of my punk-ass attitude on investors, stock prices, and the Valley's mercurial moods.

I'd never realized how much my behavior mattered. I'd always thought my work could—and *should*—speak for itself. But I'd learned the hard way that how I handled things mattered mightily. I didn't have to like it. I didn't have to agree. But I did have to deal with it if I intended to stay in this business.

And for all that work, I was lost and alone on the North Atlantic. The money, the connections, the pseudo-fame, the illusion of power...none of it could help me now. I was the only one who could help me. I was on my own here.

The nav system was on the fritz, the electrical panel was shooting sparks, and in trying to find the flashlight, I walked straight into the stainless steel server tower.

It had been almost twenty years since I'd sailed. Now, with blood running down my face in the dark, I was failing at this, too.

And then the pirates arrived.

two

OWEN

Old Salt: n. Someone who has sailed for many years. An experienced mariner.

THERE WAS a sailing vessel in my cove.

I was reading on the porch, alone save for the Japanese beetles watching me from the other side of the screen. Contentment came in the form of drinking my beer and settling into some Whitman until I noticed a light at the mouth of the cove. I gave it a long, weary stare before setting my book down.

With annoyance growing heavy on my shoulders, I pushed to my feet. This area was remote, far outside the typical routes of the luxury yachters and sport fishermen. The only visitors in these parts were locals, and they didn't come calling at this hour of the night.

That left only two options for this vessel. It was either off course or trespassing.

Now, I didn't own the water, but all the solid ground ringing the shore belonged to me. Regardless of whether this sailor had lost his way or was looking for a quiet spot to drop anchor for the night, he'd be going through me first.

I offered my old rocking chair a baleful stare before marching out of the porch. The beetles scattered as the screen door banged shut behind me. I thundered down the narrow wooden staircase that connected my home and the adjoining lighthouse to the dock. An aging skiff was moored there, opposite an equally old lobster boat.

Before casting off, I squinted over water. The intruder was drifting closer, and making no obvious attempt at turning back or signaling for aid. These waters were protected. Endangered species lived in and around the rocky coast, and vessels with that size and hull structure would leave a wake big enough to disrupt those fragile colonies. Not that I cared about the boat, but it was also in danger. If it came much closer, it was liable to run aground and that was even worse news for the conservation zone.

Time to show this sailor the way back to open water.

"It's too damn late for this shit," I groused as I turned over the skiff's motor. I could count the hours until a new day started and I was hoisting lobster traps and ferrying the day's catch to the fish markets up and down the seacoast. But this was *my* cove, and mine alone. I'd see to its preservation, as I had for nearly two decades, even if that left me tired and cranky tomorrow.

I was tired and cranky most mornings. I blamed my temperament on the backbreaking work of being a lobsterman who was doing everything in his power to survive, but there was more. Life on the ocean wasn't easy, and as the years passed, I was more and more convinced I was destined for a solitary existence.

And that made sense. I didn't like most people and hated sharing a bed. My philosophy was simple: get in, get your business done, get out. No need to complicate matters. No reason to go hog wild with those online dating schemes. Putting my information out there, on the internet, didn't sit well with me. It seemed like a big black hole of bank accounts and sexual preferences, and I didn't want to get sucked into that garbage.

No, I preferred the order and structure of my life without any of that. People, dating, the so-called digital age—I didn't need it, not when it was easy enough to dedicate one night every now and then to random hookups outside this small town.

In, out, over.

"Oh, for fuck's sake," I grumbled when I noticed the trespassing boat's lights flicker off. That wasn't a good sign for anyone.

I circled the vessel twice, the skiff's motor puttering as I slowed. It was more than enough notice for the crew, and any seaman who knew his shit would've acknowledged my presence by now. None of this felt right.

With a huff, I tossed my buoys overboard and climbed onto the trespasser's deck. I called out to the captain, hoping for a quick chat about shoreline species conservation and directions to the nearest marina.

Instead, I found myself staring down the barrel of a shotgun.

"Welcome to Talbott's Cove," I said. "Now, lower the firearm, Captain."

"I know maritime laws, and I know I did *not* invite you aboard," a hard voice said. It was hard, but there was a quiver behind it.

In one deft movement, I had the gun in hand and ammunition tumbling to the deck. "No," I said, "you did not. However, you're drifting northwest and minutes away from running aground. If that wasn't enough, you're in an ecological preserve that's only open to small crafts. You're looking at a ten-thousand-dollar fine, and on top of that, you've fucked up my night."

I hadn't gotten a good look at the shotgun-wielding captain. It was too dark in the cloudy moonlight to see more than shapes, and the man was sheltered by the mast's shadows. But now, as he stepped forward, his eyes wide with fear, I realized a few important things.

To start off, he was injured. His forehead was split with an ugly gash, his preppy polo shirt soaked with blood, and his hands were shaking.

Next, he was strong; stronger than I'd expected for a man who let his weapon make introductions. His chest and shoulders were broad, his biceps strained against his sleeves, and his thighs were thick and powerful. His hair was light, somewhere between blond and brown, though his eyes were dark. I'd place him in his early thirties, but no more than ten years younger than my thirty-nine.

Last, I was immediately attracted to him. I couldn't articulate why I found this man pulse-quickeningly sexy, and I didn't want to dwell on that reaction either.

"You need to get out of this cove," I said. He almost recoiled at the vicious snap in my words. That was one of my many problems. I was a mean sonofabitch when I wanted to be.

The captain waved at the boat. "Power's out," he said with a pathetic shrug, "and that controls everything. Motherboard on the navigation system is fried. And..." He turned his face to the night sky. "Not enough wind to catch the sails."

I stared out at the calm sea. "What about the crew? They can't bust out some duct tape and get things back in order?"

He shook his head. "No crew," he replied. "It's just me."

Well, that made no fucking sense. A boat like this, a captain dressed like that, these were the conditions for an unreasonably large crew. The one percent didn't sail solo.

"Fine. I'll radio the Coast Guard. They'll tow you to Portland," I said, my eyes drawn to the tight white polo again. He was fit as fuck, but it was the manicured, thoughtful kind of fit. It wasn't the product of hard labor but of discipline and, most likely, a lot of money. I couldn't decide how I felt about that. Forcing my attention from his chest, I sneered at his shiny new Sperrys. "Or Bar Harbor. That's probably more your speed."

"Is that where I am?" he asked. "Maine?"

He yanked a bandana from his back pocket and pressed it to his forehead. A swell of warmth moved through me, and I itched to snatch the fabric away and care for this man myself. That was another one of my problems: for all my curmudgeonly ways, I gave a shit. I didn't know how to turn off my feelings or shutter my concern. It was always there, waiting for someone to smother. Someone to drive away with my endless desire to dote.

"You're thirty miles north of Bar Harbor," I said. "So, yes. Maine."

"Bar Harbor is the opposite of my speed." The captain chuckled, but his words spoke nothing of humor or levity. "Is there anything closer? Look, I know I'm a pain in your ass right now and I admire your loyalty to the mollusks and plovers. Honestly, I do. But you can't even imagine the ration of shit I'll get if I wander back to civilization like this." He gestured to his injured face, and then the deck. "Not tonight. Just, I...please. There has to be another way."

I couldn't help myself. "I can tow you to the town harbor."

The captain's body sagged in relief. "Thank you. Seriously. I'm a fan of conservation, and if I could've prevented it, I never would have drifted into this cove." He lifted the bandana and palpated his forehead, frowning when his fingers came away bloody. He folded the fabric in on itself before returning it to the contusion. "Any chance I'll find a grocery store open at this hour? Motel?"

I glanced at my watch, the hands glowing in the inky night. Sure, I could wake up the young couple who ran the village's one and only inn, but...No. They had a new baby.

They had enough on their hands without me banging on their door. There was no need for that.

"Unlikely," I said. I rasped out an impatient breath. There was no way this would end well. Not for me, not for my cove, not for my cock. "I have...some extra room. It's not much but you're welcome to it," I said. "Though you should know I keep my firearms under lock and key. I'll expect the same of you."

"Yes. Yes, *of course*," he replied. "I can't believe you'd do that for me. Thank you."

I waved away his comments. "It's nothing," I said. I meant it. I wasn't one for houseguests but I wasn't one for turning away folks in need either. "Just—just don't be irresponsible on the water. You're not the only one you're putting at risk, you know."

He shook his head slowly, his fingers still pressed to the injury. "I know. I'm an idiot. That's probably obvious by now," he said softly, almost to himself. "My systems failed, and I was lost and confused."

"Lost and confused is one way to put it," I said under my breath.

"I've never pulled a gun on anyone before. That's gotta count for something, right?"

"Not as much as you'd think," I replied.

"I thought you were a pirate," he continued, his words dissolving into a groan. "Last month I listened to a podcast about the rise of pirate activity around the world, and that was the first place my mind went. An idiotic place, but the first."

I laughed then. A deep, true laugh, and my houseguest's lips turned up in a rueful smile. "How about you get some gear and then you come with me? Sound good?"

"That sounds amazing," he said, his voice loaded with relief. "Thank you."

"Don't mention it," I said with a quick shake of my head.

I meant that. If he offered even one more drop of vulnerability, I was bound to wrap my arms around him and claim him as my own. And that wouldn't do. Not at all. I couldn't pour all of myself into a man who was certain to up and leave without as much as a backward glance. Just like the rest of them.

I returned to the skiff in search of a winch, and kept my back to the captain. I didn't want him to see the smitten smile tugging at my lips.

three

COLE

***Back and Fill:** v. Trim the sails of a vessel so that the wind alternately fills and spills out of them, in order to maneuver in a limited space.*

I WOKE up with a skull-ringing headache.

It took me a moment to place my surroundings, but the wash-worn linen under my head smelled of soap and sea in a rough, humble way that brought to mind the great redwood of a man who boarded my boat last night.

He'd said his name was Owen Bartlett when he ushered me to this room.

Owen of the big, capable hands.

Owen of the quiet, knowing eyes.

Owen of the "Good night, and...we'll need that head of yours looked at if it doesn't stop bleeding soon."

He didn't have to bring me back here. He could've left

me to the Coast Guard and motored away without a backward glance. He was ready to kick my ass last night, but there was kindness and generosity punching through his grouchy veneer.

I rolled out of bed, groaning as the pounding in my head intensified. I would have flopped back onto the mattress, buried my face in the pillows, and surrendered to the headache if my bladder wasn't a second from bursting. I fumbled across the hall and into the bathroom.

Once relieved, I set to washing the dried blood from my face. The cut only looked terrible, as if I was an extra on *The Walking Dead*. There was swelling, and bruising running down my nose and over one cheek. As per usual, I'd inflicted a sizable amount of damage on myself.

Staring into the mirror, I realized I was almost unrecognizable.

I'd been on the covers of countless magazines—everything from *Forbes* and *Newsweek* to *Rolling Stone* and *Nylon*—and while I wasn't as identifiable as George Clooney or Justin Timberlake, most people knew I was *someone*. A memorable face, but not memorable enough to stop traffic.

But Owen didn't have to know I was *someone*. Maybe this was my chance to be no one again, if only for a couple of days.

After showering and changing into a fresh set of clothes, I dug my glasses from my bag. The pounding in my head made it impossible to see straight. Next, I fumbled through the pockets for my phone. There were missed calls, voicemails, emails, and text messages lighting up my notification bar, and I ignored all of it. I didn't need any of that noise right now. Instead, I called the small firm that built most of the components on my boat, and requested a full complement of replacement parts.

They were extremely apologetic, even offering to send their top craftsmen out to repair my boat personally. I didn't want that. They'd work too damn fast for my purposes here, and while I didn't know much about this region, I knew a crew of custom boat fabricators from California would garner too much attention. Since they didn't want negative press any more than I did, they agreed to shipping the components and keeping this quiet.

They thought I was doing them a favor by staying low profile. They thought I was only concerned with protecting my investment in their firm rather than protecting my anonymity. It was funny how these situations worked. How people focused on the things they were getting out of an arrangement before considering how the arrangement harmed or benefited others. People were, as a matter of course, self-absorbed assholes and I knew that to be a fact because I had significant experience in the self-absorbed asshole business.

But that was all the navel-gazing I needed for today.

Next, I tapped open my secure text messaging app. I'd built it myself, and it was the only thing I trusted for communication with my team.

That forced a bitter laugh from my chest. It wasn't clear to me whether I had a team anymore. Would my successor scoop them all up in a greedy power grab but strip them of their projects and priorities, leaving them to linger in corporate purgatory? CEOs called in to replace founders had a habit of doing that. They were also known for cleaning house and firing anyone connected to the old regime. Industry reporters liked to cloak it as "establishing culture" or "realigning core value pillars" but the reality was that new leadership hated the idea of semi-loyal servants. They wanted people who'd kiss the rings and bow, and they didn't care if they terminated all senior staff and vaporized institutional knowledge in the process.

But I didn't need a staff. Not really. The next steps were all on me.

I scrolled through the messages, ignoring most of them. There was one notable exception: Neera Malik. The most amazing thing about Neera was that she didn't need me. She wasn't hitching her wagon to my stars, she had no interest in climbing over me, and she was competent to the extent that I knew she'd solve most world issues if someone gave her a crack at them.

Honestly, I was just waiting for the day when the United Nations called her up and requested her immediate presence to address global hunger, or broker some peace deals. And she'd have that shit managed within a few weeks. She was actually that good.

She was also one tough motherfucker but too stoic and reserved in her motherfucking for most to notice. Her story was simple, and more uncommon than anyone wanted to believe. Born in South Carolina shortly after her family emigrated from India. Grew up poor and socially isolated. Went to Stanford on a patchwork quilt of grants, scholarships, work-study, and loans. Odd jobs at odder start-ups in the Valley for a few years. Back to Stanford for business school. Found herself the unlikely right hand to a tech giant CEO after he judged her team in a case study competition and hired her on the spot. She left him and his company in better shape than either deserved, and then moved on to me shortly before my IPO.

None of that happened every day, and there was no underestimating Neera's drive and grit. She was proper like a white-shoe law firm, and had a knack for distilling issues down to their most essential parts. Whatever *the thing* was, she knew it long before anyone else and she knew how to tell me that without sending me into fits of rage.

Neera also knew how to tell me that the fits of rage had to stop, and—magically—imparted that information without bringing about another fit of rage. She gave it to me straight, and I appreciated that. We didn't pussyfoot around.

At one point—ages ago—there was chatter of us being romantically involved after we'd attended some local events together. But not *together* together. We simply traveled in the same vehicle and people assumed we were fucking in the back seat and boardroom. We had a good laugh at that.

Neera knew I was gay, but it wasn't the talk of the town. I didn't hide my sexuality when asked about it directly, but I didn't want it to precede me. I didn't want to be the gay CEO, the gay guy in tech's (mostly) straight guy world, the one who should expect interviews to include questions about coming out rather than the company's newest innovations. I didn't want my dick involved in my business, and that meant making sure my dick was no one's business.

As for Neera, I still didn't know who or what did it for her. Aside from offering the basics of her background, she didn't share many details from her private life. I took most of my clues in that area from her. Really, I took most of my clues in all areas from her.

So, I had to respond to her message.

Neera: May I ask: where are you?
Cole: The Atlantic.
Neera: That's a vast area.
Cole: The American side.
Neera: Still vast.
Cole: I've been gone for less than a week. I'm no Magellan but I don't think I could've sailed from New York to Brazil in that time.
Cole: The most logical explanation is that I'm somewhere in the northeast Atlantic, and I'm comfortable leaving it at that.
Neera: Do I need to have you tracked?
Cole: I'd love to see you try.
Cole: As if I haven't buried everything traceable beneath thousands of redirection layers.
Cole: It would take any in-house team months to peel it all back and even then, it's not like I'm on public Wi-Fi.
Neera: Very well.
Neera: Do you have an idea as to when you'll be returning to California?

Cole: Has my presence been requested?
Neera: Your presence is always appreciated.
Cole: That is not accurate, and you know it.
Neera: I'd beg to differ.
Cole: Wait. Does the new boss expect me to show up for morning huddles?
Cole: Because fuck that shit.
Cole: I haven't seen a job description for the Chief Innovations Officer but I'm pretty sure I can't innovate if I'm wasting away in huddles and structured conversations with rigid agendas.
Cole: If you so much as mumble the words "dilemma protocol" or "wagon-wheel consultancy" I will burst into flame right now.
Neera: That sounds like a lot of effort. Save the flame for another day.
Neera: You know the team enjoys when you spend time on campus.
Cole: The team is a little over 57,000 people and the campus is roughly the size of a Hawaiian island.
Neera: Perhaps the smaller one, yes.
Cole: They don't all enjoy me.
Neera: So, you're still dissatisfied with the organizational shifts. Understandable.
Cole: Dissatisfied isn't the word that comes to mind.
Neera: Understood.
Cole: I'll keep you posted. All right?
Neera: Yes. Please do.

I BLEW out a breath and powered down my phone. My belly was rumbling, and I figured it was time to show my face. I wandered down the seaside home's hallway in search of my host. It was a long, narrow expanse of knotty pine and stone that reeked of family with its wide old hearth and country kitchen. The window over the sink was adorned with little white curtains. Tiny anchors dotted the edges, and though the embroidery's color was long since faded, they hung straight and proud, as if carefully ironed just the other day.

That was the way of this home: old, lived-in, loved.

I expected to find a rosy-cheeked woman rolling out dough for biscuits or some hazel-eyed children, perhaps a Newfoundland pup eager for a belly-scratching.

But I found none of it.

Discovering that I was alone, I helped myself to a banana. It was late in the day—I'd slept long past breakfast and lunch—and I hadn't eaten since early yesterday.

"I see you're alive."

I turned, my mouth stuffed with a chunk of banana, and saw him. A sun-bleached Red Sox cap shielded most of his face. Owen of the gravelly voice and ripped-to-fuck body.

Men like him didn't exist in my world. They just didn't look like this, not even when they worked at it. They were products of CrossFit, "clean" eating, style consultants, image strategists. And Owen couldn't compare to any of that.

Thank God.

He wasn't affected by anything other than his environment, and I figured he liked it that way.

Fuck, *I* liked it that way.

Owen pointed to my face. "Stopped bleeding," he said. "Still looks like hell."

I nodded, gulping down the banana. That left the limp peel pinched between my fingers, and while I should've been focused on disposing of it, I couldn't tear my eyes off Owen. The hair poking out from under his ball cap was dark, nearly black, with a hint of white at the temples. His eyes shone green, and his skin was dark and freckled from endless hours in the sun.

"Yeah, well..." I said, my voice trailing off. I didn't know what to say but I wanted to keep talking with him.

"Do you think you need a doctor?" he asked.

I lifted my hand to my forehead but then realized I was still holding the damn banana peel. "No, no," I said. "It's fine. I'm fine. Everything's fine."

Owen chuckled, and his shoulders lifted along with the deep chest rumbling. "You're sure about that?"

I wasn't sure. I had a business to reclaim and new programming ideas to test, but for the first time since high school, I wanted to slow it all down. I wanted to take a break.

Not the bullshit PR cover-up sabbatical, but a vacation. In Maine.

With a fisherman who didn't know anything about me.

"Yeah," I replied. "I'm good. Really good."

"Right."

Owen drew his fingertips over the dark scruff on his

jawline, and shook his head as he watched me for a long moment. I had no idea what he was thinking, but I wanted to know. I wanted to know everything.

Grumbling under his breath, he crossed the room in long strides and plucked the peel from my hand. He called over his shoulder, "How about I give you that ride down to Bar Harbor now?"

No. *No.* This was crazy. Even if he looked like rough-palmed sex, he was straight. Probably. Maybe. Aw fuck, I couldn't tell. The longer I thought about it, the easier it was to convince myself that he was gay and a huge, husky gift to me from the sea. From Poseidon himself. But it wasn't like I had enough game to make anything happen. I'd earned my born-again virgin chip some time ago.

"I'm trying to keep a low profile," I started. He was in front of me again. Close enough to touch. Definitely close enough to pick up the scent of salty air and sunscreen. *Oh, Jesus, take me now.* "Is there any chance you'd rent that room?"

Owen crossed his arms over his chest, and the grim line of his mouth turned firm.

"There's what—five, six more weeks until the end of summer? What would that run? About thirty grand?" I fumbled for my wallet, knowing I had cash in there. "I don't have it all, but here's a couple hundred, a decent deposit."

At that, Owen laughed. It was a startled, uncomfortable sound. I wasn't making a great case for myself, what with me waving a fistful of cash around. I was desperate, and that much was obvious.

"More?" I asked. "That's not a problem. What's the going rate in this region? Whatever it is, I'll triple it. I don't want to take advantage."

I knew summer shares weren't cheap. I'd buy the whole fucking house—the town—if I could stay here. And stay with him. Even if that was more ill-fated than my attempt at sailing solo. Regardless of whether Owen was as straight as a mainsail and wouldn't give me a second glance, I needed to stop being Cole McClish, boy genius, tech wunderkind, dethroned CEO. Just for a little while.

"Put your money away," Owen warned.

His voice was deep and low, all coarse vibrations that I was hungry to hear against my skin. It was absurd to think he'd reciprocate, but that didn't stop me from wanting. From hoping.

"Look, that came out all wrong. My boat is in bad shape. You saw it. It probably needs a system overhaul before I can get out of the harbor. The replacement parts, they have to be custom ordered from a small supplier in California. They're a niche operation, and let's just say they aren't up to full capacity yet. And I'm going to need some specialized tradespeople who can handle the electrical work. It's a complicated situation," I said, holding my palms out in front of me.

Owen yanked the cap off and ran his hand through his hair. He blew out a breath and tossed the cap on the butcher block countertop. "Are you running from something?" he asked.

"No," I said with a forced laugh.

Most definitely. I'm running from the reality that I'm not meant to manage the day-to-day affairs of the company I founded. I'm running from the failure of my latest project, and the failures of five before that one. I'm running from the fear that I might have lost the vision that launched my career. I'm running from all the mistakes I can't seem to shake. I'm running from the cliché of being a sad, lonely boy billionaire.

"Of course not," I continued.

Owen wasn't buying it. "You're not in trouble with the law?" he asked. "Or...something like that? Crazy ex-wife? Child support?"

I knew it then, with absolute certainty. Whether he liked me or loathed me was a direct response to this stripped down version of myself. My money, my relative fame, my history—none of those factors could cloud his perspective. I had a blank slate.

"No. None of that. Not at all," I said. It sounded believable this time. "I'm taking some time to reevaluate my business and my priorities, and wanted to get off the grid. I'd be doing that right now if my navigation and electrical hadn't shit the bed." I gestured to him, my gaze as honest as I could manage given my lies of omission. "I'm serious about paying you."

Owen looked around, his eyes prowling over every surface in the kitchen save for me. I wasn't sure whether he was debating with himself or evaluating whether I'd fucked up the precise order of things in here. He was a right-angle enthusiast. Everything just so.

"I'm not going to take your money," he said at last. He scrubbed his palm over the back of his neck, and oh what fresh hell was this life. I needed to feel *my* hand on his neck right now. "But I could use some help."

Please say you need help massaging away some knots in your neck, or a charley horse.

"You name it," I said. I was really rooting for that charley horse. Maybe we could get to the bottom of the gay/straight question, or unbox some bi-curious feelings.

"My deckhand leaves for school this week," Owen said. "He goes to the University of New Hampshire. It's early, but he works in the dorms now. Some kind of advisor. He found out about this a few days ago. Or, he *told* me a few days ago. He's a bonehead, so good luck to UNH with him."

I blinked, not sure I understood my place in this story. "You need a deckhand?" I asked eventually.

I knew he worked on the water. Hell, there was a coffee table fashioned from a lobster trap in the other room. An anemometer on the back deck. Framed photos of boats and crews decked out in yellow rain gear lined the hallway walls. Curtains embroidered with anchors. Throw pillows in the shape of seashells. This place was fisherman central.

"Yeah," he replied. "Think you can handle that?"

"I'm better with..." What the fuck did I do well? I was terrible with people, moody as shit, and hated matters of business and finance. I could code, and had the personal phone numbers of several other billionaires who alternately wanted to kill me and commiserate with me. "Technical things."

His eyebrows arched. "You had a tough time with the technical things on that boat of yours."

"Ah, yeah," I said, rubbing my temples. "Different kind of technical."

"Decking isn't hard. You'll learn," Owen said. His gaze landed on me for a long beat, and I would've fidgeted under his watch if I hadn't enjoyed it so much.

Fuck yeah, I'll learn.

"How about a steak?" He moved to the refrigerator and then the pantry, piling food and dishes in the crook of his thick arm as he went.

Soon he had the materials laid out on the counter in neat rows. All right angles. I wanted to ask how often he cooked for two, whether there was someone special in his life. This wasn't a bachelor pad. It was a *home*, a place soaked with family, comfort, tradition. The idea of Owen living here by himself filled me with sorrow. He didn't even have a dog to keep him company.

Maybe there was someone, and he saw no reason to share that information with me right now. Fair enough. It wasn't as though I was being transparent about my life either.

"Why won't you let me give you any money?" I asked from the opposite side of the kitchen island.

Owen was busy seasoning the meat, and didn't look up when he spoke. "It's not necessary," he said. "If you really need to get rid of thirty grand, give it to the Maine Lobster Conservancy."

"Is that what you fish?" I asked. Watching Owen prepare food was like ballet, but instead of the dancer and *Swan Lake*, it was a hot fisherman and red meat. Breathtaking. "Lobster?"

He nodded, and pointed his elbow toward the romaine lettuce. "Can you manage a salad? Are you as reckless with kitchen knives as you are with shotguns?"

I sighed as I reached for the cutting board and salad bowl. I wasn't living that one down any time soon. "Since we've established you're not a pirate, I'll be fine."

"Arrrrr," he barked in a stunningly bad pirate voice. I wedged in beside him at the counter and chopped the lettuce. "Ye can't be sure."

four
COLE

Spindrift: *n. Spray blown from the crests of waves by the wind.*

"SO, AH, IT'S COLE," Owen started, "right?"

I set the plates on the table and glanced up at him. "Yeah," I said, a whip of defensiveness in my words. There was no reason for it, other than my harebrained attempt at pretending to be anyone but myself.

Owen placed the salad bowl on the center of the table and pulled large wooden spoons from his back pocket. He'd tucked them there when we'd gathered the dishes and cutlery in the kitchen before transporting everything to the porch. "Just Cole? Like Cher? Or Rihanna?" He peered at me. "I guess you could make that work."

He sat at a small, weathered table, and I followed. My last name was stuck in my throat, thick and paralyzing like a mouthful of too hot coffee. The miserable part was that the coffee had to go somewhere—I had to swallow or spit—even if both options were equally unpleasant.

"McClish," I said quickly. It was more of a croak, a rough, guttural sound that I'd never be able to intentionally re-create.

Owen nodded, and busied himself with dressing the salad. I braced for the impact of recognition, the ten-second delay in which he'd put the pieces together and wonder aloud where he'd heard that name before. And then I'd be screwed.

"All right then, Cole McClish," Owen said as he heaped servings of salad, potato, and steak on our plates. He waved at me, an indication that I should eat. "This is a nice salad. Pretty spiffy how you cut those cucumbers."

"Yeah," I mumbled, staring at a forkful of lettuce and tomato. "Glad you like it."

Owen bobbed his head as he chewed. "Mmhmm."

He didn't offer another word. Not even a murmur. He really, *really* didn't know me. I couldn't believe that I had this incredible gift, this moment to be the version of myself that I wanted instead of the one I'd become, and I was experiencing it with a man too fascinating and desirable to be real. A breath whooshed past my lips, fast and ragged like I'd taken a kick to the chest. I covered it up with an exaggerated cough, and then dug into my dinner.

I worked hard at keeping my gaze trained on my plate as I didn't want to stare at my host. I mean, I *wanted* to stare and there was a whole lot of goodness to stare at, but I was still treading water here. I didn't know Owen and—as I'd discovered—he didn't know me, and that meant I had to exercise some of those manners Neera beat into me.

"Beautiful, isn't it?" Owen asked, shaking me from my thoughts.

"Yes," I agreed automatically. I'd been staring at the crescent-shaped cove without seeing, my thoughts deep in debate over whether he hauled in those lobster traps shirtless. God, I hoped so.

"I don't have a lot of material requirements," he continued, "but I don't think I could live here without a porch." He pointed his beer bottle at the floor-to-ceiling screens that separated the deck from the elements. "You just can't appreciate this view from indoors."

I wiped my hands on a napkin and tucked it beside my plate. "How long have you lived here?"

Owen sipped his beer, his head moving from side to side as if he was digging back through memories to find the start of his life in this remote corner of the world.

"A little more than fifteen years now," he said. He leaned out of his chair, jerking his chin in the direction of the slim lighthouse nestled into the high point of the cove. "One family maintained the lighthouse for almost two hundred years. The DaSilvas. They worked on the water, of course. But the younger generation wasn't interested in the upkeep. Didn't want to get involved with lobstering either." He rubbed his chin, pausing for a beat. Owen stared at the rocky cove as he spoke, and his words cooled with a bit of melancholy. "I know it's not for everyone, but it's not right for traditions to die out like that."

"Is lobstering a family tradition for you?" I asked.

"No, not my family, but I seem to think anyone who

has lived on these shores has a bit of it in their bones," Owen said.

I nodded though I didn't understand his logic. The world wasn't composed of people who felt compelled to follow their parents' footsteps anymore. There was no occupation-via-birthright.

"My mom was a high school guidance counselor before she retired. My dad worked in logging before he lost his hand," he continued. He offered a half smile with that tidbit, and I had to fight back an uncomfortable laugh. "Everyone who works in logging long enough loses something. Thankfully, it wasn't his head."

"I can understand why you wouldn't follow in his footsteps," I said. "The desire to keep your limbs and all. How did you get into lobstering then?"

"I bought this land, and the boat, from the last lobsterman in the DaSilva family," Owen said. "He took me on as a summer deckhand when I was twelve, and taught me everything." He met my gaze. "It's important work. Most people don't think much of it, but it's important to care for the sea." He gestured to the lighthouse again. "Times might change, but some things should remain the same."

"And it's only you here?" I asked, tempting him to tell me there was more to his life than lobsters and screened-in porches. He nodded. "For the past fifteen *years*? That's insanity. I'd lose my fucking mind if I was alone this much. Do the walls respond when you talk to them, or is the conversation one-sided?"

"I like it that way," he said, each word rougher than the

one before. "I enjoy being alone." He stared at me, his eyes narrowed in warning. "I prefer quiet. I hope that's not a problem for you."

I bobbed my head, in agreement or acceptance or some acknowledgement that I wasn't to question Owen's life choices any further. I was the guest here, and if I wanted to stay a guest, I'd shut the fuck up.

So much for those manners.

"The work on your vessel," he started, his voice low and heavy, "it will take weeks? Or months?"

Thanks to the kindness of the harbormaster, my boat was docked in Talbott's Cove's marina. Despite my willingness to pay above the market rate for his trouble, he rented the slip for pennies. I didn't understand this town or these people.

"Weeks," I replied, but quickly thought better of it. I was forever overcommitting on outcomes, underestimating timelines. "Although that depends on a few factors. It won't take too long to get the parts, and I think I can do some of the work myself—" Owen snorted. It was as if he knew I had a history of over-promising, too. "I'll have to hire contractors for the electrical system. There's no telling how long that could take."

Owen looked out at the water, nodding slowly. "All right."

After that, we ate in silence, the only sounds coming from waves lapping against the shore and beetles hissing as they doddled around the exterior lights. We cleared the table, and then washed and dried the dishes without sharing a single word. Once the kitchen was tidy—and right angled—Owen headed to the porch, book in hand.

He stopped at the door, his head turned in my direction but his eyes cast down. Avoiding me. "We hit the water before sunrise," he said. "Four fifteen. Be ready."

With that, the door snapped shut behind him. The message was clear: I wasn't to follow.

I heeded that message, but I also lurked in the kitchen. The view from the window over the sink allowed me to watch as Owen settled into a chair, swept his gaze over the horizon, and thumbed open his book.

So many contradictions in one man. He craved solitude but offered me—a stranger as strange as they came—a temporary home. He grunted and growled as his primary means of communication but stocked his bookshelves with great works of literature *and* read them. He believed in tradition but didn't seem concerned with passing his on to another generation.

I studied him for several minutes, and debated joining him out there. But I knew that urge was selfish—I wanted to be close to him. Figure him out. Crawl inside his mind. Then, crawl into his lap.

Instead, I returned to the room where I'd slept last night. I closed the door behind me and pivoted in a slow circle, taking in the red, white, and blue quilt, whitewashed pine walls, and rustic chest of drawers.

I wasn't special here. I wasn't gifted or talented, or remarkable in any way save for my ability to fuck things up. Part of me wanted to leave. Order a private plane to the nearest airstrip and get the fuck out of this small town before Owen realized he was better off without a roommate.

But another part—a bigger, hungrier part—wanted to stay. To be here and be no one in particular. To live like a regular person.

I stripped down to my boxer briefs and slipped between the sheets. I needed to rest up if I was going to work on a lobster boat first thing tomorrow.

five
OWEN

***Red-to-Red:** adv. The condition in which two sea-going ships traveling in opposite directions pass each other on their port sides*

COLE DIDN'T KNOW the first thing about fishing.

That was obvious when I found him inspecting my traps before sunrise this morning. He'd opened and closed them, studying the mechanism like he'd never encountered anything like it, or he thought I'd be quizzing him later.

I couldn't understand why someone who didn't know fishing or boating would set out on a solitary sailing journey. The fact that he hadn't crashed that boat of his into any underwater rock formations or another vessel was nothing short of miraculous. And he'd been out there all alone. None of it made sense to me. I didn't know what he did for a living—he'd said he owned a firm that was "in tech" and left it at that, though he indicated he had enough flexibility to take an extended summer vacation.

Must be nice.

I'd watched him from the house, leaning against the kitchen sink while sipping coffee. Barely two days had passed and I was in over my head with this man. Never mind the fact that everything inside me ached when I was around him, but he pushed me. He found my soft spots and zeroed right in.

Maybe it only seemed that way. Maybe I was overly sensitive after Cole's comments about my life of sea and solitude. And maybe I was drowning in my own needy, hungry hormones.

I'd tucked that thought away, right along with the erection throbbing behind my zipper, and went to work. I knew what I was doing when I was out on the water, and not even the presence of this beautiful man and his questions could shake my focus.

But then he fell overboard.

"I sure as shit hope you're better at those technical things," I said as I reached out to grab his hand. How he'd fallen was a mystery to me. All I knew was that he was on the deck one minute and in the water the next.

"I am," he snapped as he gained his footing on the deck. He bent at the waist, his hands propped on his knees, and took several ragged breaths.

I fisted my hands to keep from touching him. I didn't know what else to do with myself. I wanted to skim my fingers down his chest, feel the rasp of his scruffy jaw against my palm, brush the salt water from his skin, strip away his soggy clothes. "What the hell happened? Do you need to wear a life vest? You know, you seem to have a lot of accidents."

Cole gestured to the horizon. "It's choppy out here," he said. "I lost my balance when you pulled to the left."

The breeze was stirring up some whitecaps, but they were wimpy. "Just wait until hurricane season hits," I said with a laugh. "You'll understand *choppy* then."

"Fantastic," Cole grumbled. He looked down at his soaked shirt, another slim-fitting polo with an alligator over his heart, and shook his head. Then, because the deities loved and hated me in equal measures, he peeled off the offending shirt.

Fuck me.

All the humor in my body dried up and blew away. *Poof.* Gone. In its place—and the place of every other emotion I could summon—was desire. Stick-to-your-ribs, prickle-the-back-of-your-neck, hot-and-sweaty-all-over, headboard-banging desire.

Cole stood there, his legs braced and his chest bare, and wrung the ocean from his shirt while I watched. In all honesty, I was gaping. It was rude and gratuitous, and I had a schedule to keep, but I couldn't stop myself.

He was blond and golden in a way that reminded me of Zack Morris, *Endless Summer* movies, and The Beach Boys. Freckles dotted his shoulders. There was a thick patch of hair on his chest, and a fuzzy trail running between his washboard abs. His shorts were dripping wet and plastered to his legs, and my chest swelled at the giddy hope he'd take those off too.

"Any chance you have an extra shirt lying around?" Cole asked, meeting my gaze. "I realize that I've demanded quite of a bit of your hospitality, what with requiring another rescue on top of everything else, but I'd be extremely appreciative."

I blinked at him. Twice. Gulped, and then cleared my throat. "What?" I asked.

Cole swept his hand down his torso. "My shirt is wet," he said, careful to enunciate each syllable. "Do you have one I could borrow?"

A growl unfurled in my throat. "What about your shorts? Those are wet, too."

He glanced down, shrugging. "An astute observation, Owen. But I didn't figure you'd have an entire wardrobe on board," he replied.

My previous deckhand, the college kid, didn't talk much. He knew the routine and did his job with limited commentary, and we both enjoyed that approach. He had his big-ass headphones and a steady stream of whatever the kids were listening to these days, and I had the waves, the wind, the radio. It worked for us. It worked for *me*.

But now I had Cole, and he came with an endless supply of questions—he wanted to know every little thing about lobsters, fishing, boats, oceans, tides, and Maine—and chatter. All these quips and smartass comments flew at me like a swarm of greenheads in July, and I couldn't keep up because I was busy imagining the taste of his skin.

And praying that he was gay. Hell, I'd be happy with

bisexual. I'd scrub the memories of all those pretty young bi boys I'd met in Bar Harbor and Kennebunkport over the years. The ones who sucked cock like they'd declared it their major. The ones who preferred to sneak around because their parents wouldn't understand. The ones who only wanted to play in secret, the ones who led straight lives, the ones who were all for equality but refused to see themselves in the Pride flag. The ones who always went back to Yale or Penn, and their girlfriends, come September. The ones who returned summers later for their posh, picturesque weddings to those same Ivy League girlfriends. The ones who taught me to stick with one-night stands and no last names because my heart was too tender for anything real.

Yeah, I'd forget all the promises I'd made myself.

And it wasn't about being bi or pan or any other identity. It was about the shame that came with being a summer vacation secret. If Cole was any shade of queer, I'd be all over him. I'd be his.

When I didn't respond, Cole continued. "No sweat. I'm SPF'd. I can go without a shirt," he said, clapping his hands together.

I finally found my words, and they were harsh and low. "We have a schedule to keep," I said. "And we could do with less drama, McClish."

He held his hands out and quirked his brows up as if to say *Who, me?* He was cute when he wasn't busy wielding a shotgun or indulging his quarter-life crisis. He was charming in a half-smiling, eye-twinkling, chatty-Chad way. If I didn't keep my jaw clenched and my words to myself, there was no telling what would happen.

No, that wasn't true. Inaccurate. Erroneous. Completely false.

I knew what would happen. I'd laugh. Smile. Maybe even blush. I'd bend to Cole's light like a tulip to the sun, and for a few blessed moments, everything would be perfect.

But it wouldn't last. None of this would last, and it didn't matter that I had no idea what *this* was.

Cole crossed the deck and collected the hook-headed pole used to grab hold of the trap lines. He turned, the warm sunlight celebrating every line and curve on his chest, and a noise slipped from my lips. I couldn't hear much over the pulse pounding in my head but it sounded like *Ohhh-mmm-ahhh*.

"I'll grab this one," he called. He leaned over the edge of the boat, his taut body stretching as he yanked the buoy closer. It was a thing of beauty, and it would have been a glorious moment if Cole wasn't seconds away from taking another dip in the ocean. He still didn't understand how to keep himself balanced against the weight of water.

I raced to his side but it was already too late. He lost his leverage and pitched overboard trying to regain it.

"Fuck me," I muttered under my breath.

Cole swam to the surface and shook the water from his hair. "I don't know what happened there," he said.

He looked up at me with bright eyes as if he was unaware that he'd upended my life in the short days since his arrival. As if he could take a header into the water—

twice—without me wanting to spank and then swaddle him. As if he didn't know I'd spent the past two nights squeezing my eyes shut and forcing my brain to focus on anyone but him while bringing myself to silent, unsatisfying orgasms. As if I could survive this newfound companionship without coming apart at the seams.

"I don't know how any of this happened," I said through a sigh.

six

COLE

***Arc of Visibility:** n. The portion of the horizon over which a lighted aid to navigation is visible from seaward.*

THIS TOWN—IF you could call the tiny collection of homes, boats, and roads that—was charming. Small and storybook quaint, and humble. The people here were decent, honest, salt of the earth. All the things snotty dickheads like me said about people who lived simply and worked the land and sea.

And no one gave a shit about me. At least that was how I was interpreting the reception I'd received in the past few days. The folks in town were curious about Owen's houseguest, sure, but they were more interested in my boat than my origins or identity. The sailors and fishermen in the area wanted the lowdown on my vessel, and they accepted me without qualification.

I couldn't decide whether I'd overestimated my

celebrity or underestimated the allure of a beautifully crafted sailboat. It had to be some combination of both.

That, and the realization that Silicon Valley was a weird little jungle gym composed of ambition and backstabbing, gossip, and crazy wild money. We in the Valley—and sometimes, California as a whole—liked to believe we had it right. We knew the way, and everyone else just had to hurry the hell up. But living in Talbott's Cove and working the decks forced me to reconsider all that. I was beginning to believe that this was right, and the Valley was missing out on something essential.

It was a learning experience, this past week with Owen. We were both particular, but Owen erred on the side of anal retentive perfectionism, and I didn't understand that shit. I was a night owl, and I figured a lifetime on the water had formed Owen into an early bird. He was a Red Sox fan, and—apparently—I was wrong.

But it was a good week. *Great* week. I learned things I'd never considered—separating lobsters based on size and sales channel, tying knots for every conceivable purpose, maintaining a lighthouse—and basked in the warmth of Owen's approval every time I got it right. He was an antisocial grump to be sure, but that didn't make him any less of a good man. And he was *good*.

When finished hauling in his lobsters for the day, Owen turned his attention to fishing tuna, haddock, cod. He sold some directly to restaurants along the coast, but he delivered most of it to a farm-to-table co-op program that distributed fresh fish to nursing homes, veterans' hospitals, and public schools. He was a member of the Talbott's

Cove town council because—according to Owen—he wasn't going to let some yahoos take over.

The guy practiced what he preached, and there was something about that—about being a man who I could respect and admire—I found devastatingly sexy. I had to drag my gaze away from his thick, powerful arms every time he pulled a trap up from under the sea. Or when he planted his feet wide on the deck, his shoulders tight and his long stare traveling over the water like he was a ruler appraising his kingdom.

Owen was strong and sure, and I wanted him. In every possible way.

If I was even half as strong or sure as Owen, I would've told him I was attracted to him. I would've told him I wanted to kneel at his feet and rub my cheek on his thighs, and beg for the privilege of serving him.

But I wasn't, and I didn't.

I rationalized it all away as fear of wrecking the good things I had going here, but that wasn't it. I was afraid of rejection. *His* rejection. I preferred to be the one who did the rejecting—as fucked up and shallow as that was—and I didn't know how to make the first move.

Oh, I thought about those first moves. Thought about them all the fucking time.

The old stretch-an-arm-around-the-shoulder bit while watching television. Some flirty dinnertime chatter about how he liked his meat. Another fall overboard—intentional this time—and another excuse to peel off my shirt.

I mentally choreographed every one of those moves, but never executed any of them. The rejection would kill me, and kill this idyllic break from my reality. Instead, I followed Owen everywhere he went. Less lost dog, more cat in quiet heat. It was painful, all this self-denial, but Owen declining my advances would hurt more.

The worst part was the ticking clock. The knowledge that my time in Talbott's Cove was limited. Work on my boat was slow and spendy, but it would end right along with the summer. Not that I brought up my departure, and Owen didn't ask.

———

Neera: Any update on your expected return date?
Cole: Not that I have planned, no. I believe I was instructed to take the summer. My understanding of meteorological summer is that it ends on September 1. If we're talking astronomical summer, it ends on September 22.
Cole: Thusly I won't consider a return until sometime between or after those dates.
Neera: Are you still on the Atlantic?
Cole: Is my name still on the masthead as founder?
Neera: I sincerely hope that isn't a serious question.
Cole: Wasn't sure how quickly things would change.
Neera: You're exceptionally argumentative.
Cole: If that's what you want to call it, fine, but I'm just doing what you recommended. I'm out of the picture, not making noise or starting problems, and I'm not interfering with my replacement.
Cole: I can't see how that's problematic.

Neera: It's not. I only wanted to get a sense of your timing so I could best support your return.

Cole: I'm working on something new. I don't want to talk about it yet but I'll keep you looped in when I have something to share.

Cole: Does that work?

Neera: I'll make it work.

seven

COLE

__Slack Tide:__ n. A short period when the water is completely unstressed and there is no movement in the tidal stream, before the direction of the tide reverses.

"MAY I JOIN YOU?" I asked, leaning through the doorway to the porch.

Owen was kicked back in his chair, a book in his lap and a tumbler of whiskey by his side. If there wasn't an interesting ball game to watch after dinner, Owen often settled on the porch and I holed up in my room. I'd made good progress with a handful of new ideas I was testing out, but I was climbing the walls tonight.

I didn't mind the routine we had going here—awake before dawn, on the water all morning, fish markets followed by work fixing up my boat in the afternoon, dinner around sunset, bed shortly after—but I needed something more tonight. Back in California, most of my days were spent talking. Taking calls, sitting in meetings, hearing from my coders, arguing with my board. There was always someone or something that required my attention, and being here with Owen was still strangely quiet for my tastes.

Gesturing to the open seat beside him, Owen said, "Yes, but I have some conditions."

I stepped onto the porch, thankful for the slight drop in temperature from the heart of the house. The air was still heavy and thick, the day's heat and humidity continuing long after sunset. Only the slightest breezes blew in off the water, and they were laced with the pungence of seaweed and marsh.

"Anything," I said, dropping into the open rocking chair. Before coming to Talbott's Cove, I would've ascribed rocking chairs to grandmothers and nurseries, and nothing much else. But these were just right.

"No questions," Owen said. I bit back a groan at that. "You've asked all the questions necessary, and I need a break." I opened my mouth to reply, but he held up his hand. "No. No, this isn't an opportunity to ask why. Just live with it."

"I'll try," I said, rocking back in the chair. I could see why Owen enjoyed this. It was just like being on the water. "It would be really terrible if I died of curiosity though."

Owen snarled and set his book on the table beside him. "How would that even happen, McClish?"

I held out my hands, shrugging. "I can think of a

number of ways," I started, "but I'll keep them to myself. I don't want to bother you."

He hissed out a breath and I was convinced he grumbled, "Oh, for fuck's sake."

I had to suck my lips between my teeth and bite down to keep from laughing. "We don't need to talk," I said. "We've got the ocean and the stars, and there's no need to talk. This is great. You do you, Bartlett."

I glanced over at him. He was sighing and grumbling as if I was causing him physical discomfort. At least he couldn't turn himself on with those sounds. I did not possess the same immunity. With my hands folded over my crotch as casually as I could manage, I gazed out over the water and focused on identifying all the constellations I could find. It was good, distracting work, and it would've kept me distracted if not for Owen's huffing and snarling.

Such a moody one, this Owen Bartlett.

"All right," he said, finally breaking free of his sigh-a-thon. "How would one *die* of curiosity?"

"Marie Curie comes to mind," I mused. I leaned forward, my arms braced on my thighs, and studied the Japanese beetles congregating on the screens. The yellow glow of the porch's overhead light attracted them, but the screens held them off. They were small, pea-sized, but their low hiss called to mind the sound of old-fashioned dial-up. I imagined they were sweltering, too.

"How do you figure?" Owen snapped. "She discovered radium."

"Oh, yes, and polonium," I agreed. "It killed her."

He reached for his whiskey and took a hearty gulp. "Right. You're not discovering new elements tonight."

"And the cat." I sat back, nodded toward him.

The lighthouse blinked on the far end of the cove, the brightness illuminating his features. My fingers ached to trace the scruffy line of his jaw, stroke my thumb over his cheeks, scratch my nails along his scalp. My skin was flushed from the unrelenting heat but now I was *hot*. Hungry, too.

Owen waved his glass in front of him. "What cat?"

He was getting riled up, and I loved that shit. A few days ago, I pretended I didn't know the difference between flat head and Phillips head screwdrivers for the simple pleasure of his exaggerated reaction.

"The one killed by curiosity," I replied. "*That* cat. Poor bastard."

Owen sighed as he shook his head, but it morphed into a chuckle. Soon, his shoulders were shaking as he laughed. I laughed too. I couldn't help it. The deep, full-bodied sound was contagious.

"I don't know about you, McClish," he said as he patted his belly. "I just don't know."

"What do you want to know?" I asked.

We hadn't ventured into the realm of discussing more than the basics of my life, and that was good enough for me. Owen knew I owned a technology firm—didn't think it was necessary to mention that it was the biggest one in the world—and I lived in California. The rest of it was just details, and I couldn't find a reason to share them with

Owen. It wasn't that he wouldn't care or wasn't interested, but that I didn't want to spend all of our time talking about me. He and this quaint town were the most interesting things I'd ever encountered, and I wanted to soak up all of it.

He considered his whiskey for a moment before saying, "You're from California? That's where you grew up?" He sipped, and then shot me a sharp glance. "It would explain a lot."

He didn't look at me long, and that was fair. I wasn't much to look at. Bruised, swollen, blood dried black around the laceration. I rarely indulged in vanity but I wasn't accustomed to being hideous.

"I am," I said carefully. I longed for a drink to occupy my mouth and hands. I hadn't thought that far ahead before venturing out here. "But—I mean—not the California most people associate with California."

Owen regarded me over his glass, an eyebrow bent. "There are multiple Californias?"

I murmured in agreement. "Northern and Southern," I said. "But there's more to it than that. It's a collection of ecosystems more complex than anything contained within conventional notions of statehood." Both of Owen's eyebrows were arching up into his hairline now. "When people think of California, they think of Los Angeles and San Diego. Surfing, beaches, girls roller-skating in bikinis. But that's not the whole story. You have the South Coast but also the North and Central Coasts. There's the Sacramento Valley, the San Joaquin Valley, and *The* Valley. There's the Cascades, the Sierras, and the Inland Empire.

And then there are the big cities. Bay Area, Los Angeles, and San Diego."

"That was an extremely long way of telling me that California is a big place," he said. "This is why you're not allowed to talk."

I leaned toward him and rapped my knuckles on the arm of his chair. "I forgot about Orange County. Add that to the list."

"Is that where you live?" Owen asked. "Or where you're from?"

He grabbed the front of his t-shirt and fanned himself with the fabric. I thought about inviting him to take it off. Strip down. If that didn't offer enough relief, we could wade into the water and hold each other under the ripe moonlight and...*ahhhh*. I went from zero to pervert in three seconds flat.

I bobbled my head, trying to shake that idea loose. "No and no," I said, laughing to stifle a growl of desire. "Like I said, people associate California with beaches and bikinis, but that's not how it is for everyone. I grew up about three hours east of San Diego, right along the Colorado River and the Arizona border. It's hot and dry and mostly flat, and the only kind of trouble you can get into out there is stupid trouble."

"You speak from experience," Owen said. "Nearly running your boat aground isn't your first brush with being a damn fool, I take it."

Why did I enjoy this man's insults so much? I couldn't explain it, but I wanted him to keep going. Pick apart my privilege-soaked preferences and deride my expensive polo shirts. Tear down my quirky-for-the-sake-of-wonky mannerisms. Strip it all away.

"If you're asking whether I hacked into Agua Fria High's student information system and deleted all of my unexcused absences from skipping ninety percent of my calculus classes—" I held up my hands and then let them fall. "Then, yes, I might've found myself in a bit of trouble."

"Of course," Owen muttered.

"But I'll have you know," I added, "I only got caught because I took the final exam. The teacher didn't recognize me. I should've skipped that too, and then hacked back into the SIS to give myself a grade. Should've. Didn't. Me and my goddamn morals."

Owen stared at me for a long moment, his eyes narrowed and his brow crinkled. "Are there any consequences in your world, McClish?"

"There are," I said, breaking away from his gaze. "There are definitely consequences." I cleared my throat as I sneaked a glance at him. His attention was on the stars now. "Anyway, I live in Palo Alto."

"Which is in the Bay Area," Owen supplied. "Near San Francisco."

"Right," I said. "My sisters are all over the place. One in Denver, the other outside Baltimore. My mom lives in Palm Springs now. I tried convincing her to check out Balboa Island or Marina del Rey, but she prefers the inescapable heat. I only visit her in the winter. I can't deal with summer in the desert. I feel like I'm trapped in a dehydrator and turning into beef jerky."

"You'd make for some fine jerky," Owen said, laughing.

"As would you, Bartlett," I replied. There was no humor in my tone, but I couldn't hold back the smile.

"I'd gnaw on you," he continued, eyeing my torso.

My heart was in my throat, thumping fast as I tried to breathe, swallow, think.

What the actual fuck was happening here? Was he... hitting on me?

No. Of course not. This was an awkward bit of humor gone astray, not a revelatory moment where we simultaneously flashed our queer cards.

Or maybe it was exactly that moment.

"I'm not a piece of jagged, dried-out meat," I said indignantly. "I'm tender, juicy meat."

Nothing ventured, nothing gained.

"Yeah, you are. You're some fine cut of meat." Owen barked out a startled laugh and pushed to his feet. "Whoa. Okay. Now I know I'm drunk," he said. "Get some sleep, McClish. Another early day is coming our way."

I nodded and babbled something in response, but I couldn't stop hearing his words in my head. *I'd gnaw on you*. It wasn't clear what I'd gained there, but I was satisfied with the venture.

eight
OWEN

Between Water and Wind: *n. The part of the ship's hull that is sometimes submerged and sometimes above water by the rolling of the vessel.*

I CAN'T KEEP *this up for much longer. Something has to give.*

That was what I was telling myself as I stomped around the deck and growled at the sunny sky. The sky hadn't offended me in any notable way but I was in a mood. The kind of mood that could turn milk sour and burn holes in the rug without much effort. The kind of mood born from telling Cole I wanted a taste of him and then going to bed needy and alone.

But then it got worse when I saw him reeling in a trap, and leaning too far over the starboard side while he did it.

Please, Jesus, don't let him fall in. I don't possess the strength for his bare chest today.

"Keep your feet planted, McClish," I called, jerking my chin toward the starboard side buoys. The sun was high overhead, and only here, miles from the shore, did the breeze extinguish August's humidity. "If you go for a swim, you're dragging your ass out of the water this time."

"Would you shut the fuck up?" Cole replied. "I got it."

I tossed several more traps into the water while Cole wrestled one up. The first time he'd hoisted up a trap filled with live lobsters by himself, he'd fumbled it back into the water with an uncomfortable howl. Today, he was better. He knew what to expect this time, and he didn't flinch when reaching in to sort the sellable lobsters from the ones who deserved more time under the sea.

He looked better, too. The bruising on his face had cooled to a sickly yellow-green shade, and he seemed relaxed. That first night, when his boat was stalled in the cove, probably wasn't the standard by which to judge Cole McClish, but the hard work and hot sun were doing him good. I could tell, and I couldn't help but look every chance I got.

After some time in Cole's company, I'd learned a few things about the curious stranger who'd drifted into my cove. He couldn't fish worth shit but I'd admit he wasn't the worst sailor. He just ignored his instincts in favor of the nav systems and sonar. It was as if he trusted the machines more than he trusted himself. We couldn't be more different in that respect. To me, the machines were unreliable. They were bound to fail, and they'd fail when I needed them the most. I didn't want to put my faith in anything I couldn't trust completely.

He also talked all goddamn day, and his approach to tidiness was distinctly untidy. It was a damn good thing he was hotter than the sun itself because there'd be no surviving his chaos otherwise.

He was avoiding something or someone but I didn't want to know. I wasn't asking any more personal questions. I cared but I couldn't go there again. I couldn't discover that he had a woman or a family out west, or even a home to which he was eager to return. I could only manage Cole the stranger, void of context or complications. Or cute stories about his hatred of desert climates.

When he set another trap and dropped it off the side of the boat without hesitation, my chest surged with pride. He'd learned all that from me.

"You didn't even cry with that one," I said as I traversed the deck. "We'll make a lobsterman out of you yet."

I clapped him on the back at the exact moment as he pivoted toward me, and that left us in an unexpected embrace. His chest was hard against mine and he was breathing heavy and I couldn't move. Wouldn't. Wouldn't for anything.

My hand continued patting his shoulder. How could I stop? How could I push him away when the only thing I truly wanted was to feel his skin under mine?

Cole's fingers were curled around my forearm as if he was bracing himself, but instead of maintaining a polite distance, he leaned into me. His shoulder was on my chest and his breath was on my neck, and *I want you more than I've ever wanted anyone* was on my tongue.

Neither of us made a move to break away for a long, confusing beat that twisted with more heat and affection than I could handle without embarrassing myself right now. He smelled good, like sunscreen and sweat. I wanted to memorize that scent, and everything else about the way we fit together.

I didn't want that to *mean* something, but it did. It meant everything to me.

Clearing my throat, I eventually drew my hand back and gazed at the water. "Need to make some deliveries up the coast," I said, still watching the waves as I stepped away from him. I wasn't ready to look at Cole, and I didn't. I returned to the controls without a backward glance because I couldn't trust myself to meet his eyes without revealing the depth of my desire for him. "Go put that catch on ice."

―――

"THIS IS AN EXCELLENT BURGER," Cole said. "The last time I had a burger, it was made of mushrooms, lentils, and pumpkin seeds."

"That's a crime," I replied. "Tell me who did that to you. I'll make him pay."

Cole chuckled around another bite. "Plant-based eating is increasingly popular in my world," he said. "I'd forgotten that meat is delicious. I'm getting really spoiled here. And fat."

He patted the blue polo shirt over his flat belly, the one I'd seen bare too many times to forget. The afternoon sun was scorching, and once the day's catch was out of pinching range, he peeled those shirts right off. He was golden and sculpted, and I only allowed myself brief glances.

"You've been kind to let me stay here, Owen," he said. He shrugged, kicking the emotion out of this moment. "Much more of this home cooking and good conversation, and you're going to ruin your reputation as a pirate."

"Fuck off, McClish," I murmured.

A smile pulled at my lips. This companionship *was* nice. The domesticity, too. Looking after someone fed an urge that I'd otherwise ignored, and there were moments when caring for Cole satisfied me more than anything I could imagine between the sheets. I liked our dinners on the porch together, even his nonstop questions and chatter. We often sat out here long after the meal was over, drinking beer and admiring sunsets. I didn't mind that our evenings put me behind on my reading, even if I told my houseguest otherwise. Whitman could wait. Thoreau, too.

Cole tipped his beer bottle to his lips and shot an anxious glance at me. "You know...you don't have to wait on me. I won't get into trouble around here." He turned his attention to the cove before continuing. "I'm sure you have friends. A girlfriend, or you know, someone you like to spend time with. You don't have to put your life on hold because I'm hanging out at your place."

I reached into the ice chest between us and grabbed

two more longnecks. It wouldn't be Maine if you didn't have beer available indoors and out.

"I'm still worried that you're going to accidentally shoot yourself," I said, knocking the bottle caps off. Another mouthful of cold beer washed down my internal debate. I wasn't ashamed of myself, and while I didn't hide my sexual orientation, it wasn't something I offered up. I favored gay bars, Pride events, situations where it was implied. Where I didn't have to hide. Where I was with my people, my family. Not my blood relations, but my true family.

Even after more than twenty years of comfort in my queer skin, I didn't savor coming-out conversations. But I'd done basically that this afternoon, with that hug. I was still feeling every spot where his body had connected with mine. There was no mistaking the heat between us, and I couldn't be the only one feeling it.

Here goes nothing. "No girlfriends. I'm not interested in women."

Cole cocked his head to the side as if he'd misheard me. "Does that mean you prefer men?" he asked, his brow furrowed. He looked like a puppy who couldn't find his ball. "Or do you consider yourself asexual? Not that a lack of interest in women is indicative of asexuality. You could identify any number of ways. It's a spectrum."

"I'm gay, if that's what you're asking," I replied.

Cole's mouth fell open as my words registered, but he rapidly schooled his expression. "That's cool," he croaked.

Fuck. Fuck it all.

"Is that going to be a problem for you?" I asked, studying his reaction.

"No," he said.

It was a little too forceful, as if he knew he was walking the line between acceptable responses and honest ones. It would be a real shame if he was a bold-faced homophobe. Couldn't have that. I gave no quarter to the haters.

"No," he repeated, pushing his glasses up his nose. "Not at all. You just caught me by surprise." He threw his hands up, then pressed his fingers to his eyelids. "Shit, that's not the right thing to say. I don't have to prepare myself to respect anyone's sexual orientation. No one should need an adjustment period to accept another human being. It's not like you're telling me you keep a bag of your ex's old hair with you at all times."

"No worries," I said. I meant that. Eventually, there'd be a time when we led with curiosity rather than assumptions about sexual identity, race, faith, ability...all of it. But today wasn't that day, and considering I had a roof over my head, food in my belly, and the sea in my backyard, I could cope with humanity's shortcomings. "Are we good?"

"No—I mean, yes—we're cool. Yes." He scrubbed his hands over his face and then picked up his beer, gazing at the bottle like sweet salvation. "If you're seeing someone, please don't change your routine on my account. You're welcome to bring, ah, him around."

I watched his throat bob as he guzzled his beer, and while I felt better that I'd cleared the air between us, I'd be lying if I said I wasn't disappointed that he didn't offer up his own big gay announcement. That would have improved this conversation considerably. It also would've helped me understand the constant fizz and pop of tension I felt when he was nearby. It would've explained the way my body reacted to his touch today, and his starring role in all of my fantasies.

But this was the way of it for me. I was forever falling for men who had neither the room nor interest in their lives for me, then hating the world for a time. That was why I didn't do *this*. I didn't get to know men, and I didn't bring them home or let them into my world. I kept it clean and easy. A night in the city, a bar or club, a guy I'd never see again. A boozy weekend in Provincetown with a handful of bears who knew what I needed and expected nothing come Monday. It was better when it didn't mean anything to me. When I didn't care.

"I'll keep that in mind," I said, the words rough as I forced them out.

"Come on," he said, gesturing inside. "The game is starting soon, and you're miserable if you miss the first pitch."

I shook my head at that, sweeping away my dark and broody thoughts. "I like to watch the entire game. That doesn't mean I'm miserable if I miss the first pitch," I said. "That you can live on highlights alone means you were dropped on your head as a baby."

"But the games are so long," he whined.

"Baseball is meant to be appreciated in its complete form," I countered. "You need to realize that life shouldn't be condensed down to a couple hundred characters, McClish."

He stopped gathering our plates to glance at me. "Wait. Was that a Twitter reference? I thought you were taking Thoreau's *Walden* approach to life, but you're a down-low Tweep, aren't you?"

Cole extracted a great deal of pleasure from ragging on my low-tech lifestyle. "That sounded like a gay slur, McClish."

"Not even a little bit," he said, laughing as he walked to the kitchen sink. He set the dinner dishes in the basin, stacking them just as I'd instructed. "I'll wash tonight."

"I don't know anything else about Twitter," I confessed, grabbing a dish towel off the oven door handle and slinging it over my shoulder while he filled the sink with water and soap. "I don't understand what all those internet things are about, or why anyone uses them."

"Ultimately, you don't need any of them," Cole said, his hands deep in the soapy water. "It's basically a study in herd behavior."

I accepted the plate he handed me and set to rubbing it dry. "Come again?"

"Yeah," he said, running a scrubbing brush over a handful of forks and knives. "Social media is inherently dehumanizing. Most platforms peel back the artifice of human communication and reduce people down to basic instincts. There's a reason the internet is filled with porn."

"Oh," I murmured. I'd heard that, about the porn, but I was old-fashioned. I liked my dirty DVDs, and the adult toy store I frequented in Portland had a hearty supply. "That's interesting."

"People on Twitter are like cats," Cole continued. "They knock shit over because why the fuck not?"

"Seems like a great use of time," I replied.

"People on Facebook are dogs at the dog park. They're running around in circles, looking for belly rubs, and barking when they're happy, sad, angry, and confused." He handed me another plate. "People on Tumblr are raccoons. They only come out when it's dark and they love trash. There are a few on Reddit, and they're toads. They make a lot of noise and then disappear when someone wants to interact with them on a meaningful level. And the people on Instagram, they're squirrels. They love shiny things and never stop fidgeting."

"Fascinating," I said. I dried another plate and then got to work with the utensils. "You're saying there's nothing good about any of it? It's all terrible people and toxic behavior?"

"No, of course not," Cole said. He was scrubbing the sink now, and he was only doing that because I'd given him a hard time about leaving the basin dirty a few nights ago. He hadn't noticed the bits of potato or salad dressing residue, but that shit annoyed the hell out of me. "People find each other, despite geographic distance and social factors that would've otherwise kept them apart. There are communities of support and affinity, groups mobilizing for important causes, and collaboration that would've never been possible before internet access flattened and condensed the world. There are moments when the very best of humanity is on display, but there are also moments of the absolute worst. For all the good, there's plenty of bad."

"And this is how you make your living?"

"It is," Cole said with a rueful laugh. "If not for the cats and dogs, and raccoons, toads, and squirrels, I'd have nothing." He looked up and hit me with a paralyzingly sweet smile. "I certainly wouldn't be here."

"To the cats and dogs," I said, raising an empty glass.

He reached across me for one of the upturned glasses I'd set on the countertop after drying, and his arm rubbed against my abdomen in the process. It was nothing much, just a quick touch not unlike many we'd shared while washing dishes every night this past week, but it was different now.

"To the cats and dogs," Cole repeated.

I choked back a groan before he lifted his glass and we toasted a world I didn't know.

We finished cleaning up in silence and shifted toward the living room when the kitchen was in good shape. There were a couple of minutes before the game started, and Cole was surfing through the channels. He had an aversion to watching the evening news, one I didn't understand but didn't mind indulging.

"You really should let me rewire your setup," Cole said, gesturing to the footage from football's preseason training camp. "Get a DVR, and some expanded access for games outside your market. You'll appreciate it come football season."

"Sit down and enjoy the damn game," I said, pointing at the sofa.

"Every minute of it," he said. "But—one more thing. You could fast forward through commercials, you know. I can't imagine you enjoy all the promos for Canobie Lake Park and Jordan's Furniture."

"That's where you're wrong," I said. "I love that shit, and it's no secret that Water Country has the best jingle."

Cole turned to me, stone-faced. "We're going to agree to disagree on that point."

We settled into an amiable banter of cheers, groans, and curses punctuated with comfortable silence. I'd been alone for years and rarely considered what it would be like to have a partner, but playfully arguing with Cole about the Red Sox showed me what I could have. What I wanted.

The game went into extra innings, and though I wasn't built for too many late nights followed by early mornings, I wasn't interested in abandoning my position on watching the entire game. I was a stodgy bastard like that.

But Cole's hands were folded low on his belly, right above his crotch, and through the thin fabric of his athletic shorts, I could make out the shape of him. And *oh fuck*, it was a nice-looking shape.

There was nothing overtly sexual about his position, yet I yearned for the right to reach over and take my man in hand. He was close enough to touch, and I didn't think I could endure extra innings tonight with that temptation.

When it was clear the Sox were taking home an easy win, I clicked off the television and stood, brushing my palms down the front of my cargo shorts. I'd never been one for spontaneous erections, but beer and too-thin athletic shorts and this proximity to Cole brought me damn close. My cock was heavy and aching, and I needed to find some relief far away from my guest's watchful eyes.

"We'll hit the water early," I said, desperate to keep my mind on topics that didn't involve imagining the rasp of Cole's unshaven jaw against my inner thighs.

He nodded as he collected the empty beer bottles. He was meticulous about recycling, and had gone so far as to lecture me about the impact of plastics on marine life. Somehow he knew as much, if not more, about preserving the seas than I did.

"Yeah," Cole said. "That works for me."

He sounded distant, and not because he was busy tidying the kitchen. He was distracted. "Everything okay, McClish?" I asked.

He folded a dish towel into precise thirds and set it on the counter with a pat, and then glanced up with a forced smile. "Great."

I didn't know him, not well enough to read his every mood and twitch, but I had the distinct sense that he *wasn't* great. "Good," I said.

Cole patted the towel again and reached for a glass. "Yeah," he replied, watching me while he filled his glass with water. He drank it down, his eyes still trained on me.

Not unlike sitting beside him on the couch, there was nothing loudly attractive about drinking water but I couldn't save myself from the pull of his body. It was a vortex sucking me in. I wanted to touch him and taste him, and I wanted him to love it as much as I knew I would.

But that wasn't my life. That wasn't how it went for me.

"Listen, man," I said, gesturing toward him. "You can tell me if something's bothering—"

"Not at all," Cole replied quickly. "I'm preoccupied with some work issues. A lot on my mind." He tapped his temple as if to confirm the location of his troubles. They were not in his shorts as I'd hoped. "Things I'm trying to sort out. Problems, bugs. That's all." He nodded several times, and I was certain he believed the repetition was critical to convincing me. "I'm going to tackle some of that."

He patted the towel again.

"Yeah," I replied.

He moved around me, slipping down the hallway with little more than a hasty "Good night" as his chest brushed against my back. I didn't press the issue. I wanted to, but I didn't know what or how to press. And more importantly, I needed a very cold shower.

nine

COLE

Constant Bearing, Decreasing Range: *n. The condition when two vessels are approaching each other from any angle that stays the same over time. Also known as a collision course.*

Neera: You'll notify me before you do anything substantive, right?

I BARKED out a laugh when I read those words.

I'd been closed up in my small room for a matter of moments before reaching for my phone in hopes of a distraction from Owen. Not that I wanted a distraction, of course, but it wasn't like I could throw myself at him. As thrilled as I was to hear of his preference for penis, I couldn't drop my shorts and ask if he wanted a taste of mine.

It was also possible that he wasn't interested in me.

Two gay men could live under a shared roof without devolving into a fuck festival. Although it would certainly help if one of those men was up front about his sexuality when peach-ripe opportunities presented themselves.

I shook my head, astounded by my own absurdity.

Neera: Real estate purchases, public appearances, search and rescue teams, the like? I'd rather not have a repeat of the Appalachian incident.

Cole: Of course. But I'll remind you that you thought the Appalachian incident was going to be great, and the search and rescue team was totally unnecessary.

Cole: Further, I haven't gotten a haircut without your input in almost a decade.

Neera: Please don't consider this an invitation or suggestion to repeat the Appalachian incident. I can speak for the senior leadership and board of directors when I say getting lost in the Smoky Mountains at night again is ill-advised.

Cole: No, nothing Appalachian in my future. I'm quite content where I am.

Neera: And yet you won't tell me where that is, what you're doing, or when you'll be back.

Cole: Only because I'm 100% certain you'll charter a plane and come check on me.

Cole: That would be great but I need some time and space to work everything out.

Neera: Some habits are hard to break.

Cole: Like managing up?

Neera: You're allowed privacy and secrets, but you're also allowed to trust people.
Cole: I do. I trust you implicitly.
Cole: I also trust the person I'm staying with, and I want to protect that person's privacy as well.
Neera: Oh.
Neera: Okay. All right. I understand.
Cole: Let me get this straight. I'm allowed to have privacy only if it involves human companionship?
Neera: Yes, that's correct.

THAT YIELDED ANOTHER LAUGH.

I could've gone a few more rounds with Neera but I set my glasses on the bedside table, then switched my phone off and tucked it away in my duffel bag. My head wasn't in the right place to chat with her tonight. Based on my conduct earlier, I wasn't in the right place to chat with anyone.

Years ago, back when my company was first taking off, I sat for a live television interview. *Train wreck* wasn't an adequate representation of how poorly it went. I had an asshole answer for every question. I drummed my fingers on the armrest, rolled my eyes, and sighed audibly. I couldn't get comfortable in the chair so I shifted and repositioned to the point of distraction, and then snapped at the interviewer when he asked if I was all right.

That hot mess was a shining achievement compared to the way I handled Owen this evening.

All the opportunities in the world were in front of me,

and I skipped over every one of them. I could banter and bullshit all day long but that was it. That was all I had—bullshit. All systems were go, the bases were loaded, the stars were aligned...and I blew it. Not only did I blow it, I came off like an apathetic dickhead. I said all the wrong things, laughed like an idiot, and rolled deep in the awkward pauses.

It was true. I didn't know how to get out of my own way.

With a groan, I pushed off the bed and headed to the bathroom. I had to wash up for the night, and then I was determined to sleep off today's indiscretions and start anew tomorrow. I could manage that. I could even sit Owen down after we delivered the day's catch and tell him about my—

"Unnnnnnf."

I stopped in the hallway, my hand frozen an inch from the bathroom door handle, and I heard it again.

"Mmmmm."

It took only a moment to place that sound and the unmistakable rhythm of skin shuttling over skin. The air went out of my chest and everything in my body turned hot, my skin prickling with awareness because Owen was masturbating within inches of me.

A decent guy would've retreated immediately and given Owen the privacy he deserved. I wasn't that guy, and I didn't think I could move from this spot if a family of tiny purple ponies paraded down the hall and asked for directions to the carnival.

I leaned forward, closer to Owen and the noises I

wanted to memorize and keep in a special, secret place. If I couldn't invite myself into his self-love session—because I possessed *some* decency—I was going to listen real hard.

Not trusting myself to remain standing without support, I rested my forehead against the doorframe. That was when I noticed it. The door had been warped by years of close proximity to the ocean air, and shutting it all the way required a firm shove. Owen hadn't given it that shove.

Only a thin sliver of him was visible, but that was more than enough. The vanity light shone down on his dark hair, bathing him in a warm glow. His shirt was rucked up around his chest and his shorts were barely out of the way, as if he'd surrendered to this need with haste. His hand gripped the edge of the sink, his knuckles white. His other hand moved in a lightning-quick blur that demanded my cock's full attention.

I was hard and ready, and I had to make a decision. I could stand in this hallway while Owen jerked it on the other side of the door, or I could go back to my room. There was one more option, of course, but I didn't have the balls to push the door open and observe this act to completion.

"*Ohhh*," he groaned. "Oh *fuuuuck*."

There was a flash of white that obscured my view for a moment. When it cleared, I found a towel gnashed between Owen's teeth, muffling his noises. Seeing him desperate like this triggered something inside me, and before I could think better of it, my fingers were curling around my cock.

I thrust into my palm in time with Owen but my pleasure was secondary. I was only concerned with him. His movements, his noises, his need. It was glorious, and I couldn't contain my groan when he slowed to long, twisting strokes that offered a glance at his thick erection.

Owen's eyes popped open and his gaze darted to the door. He caught sight of me, and answered my groan with a gasp.

Then all the words I knew in this language flew out of my mouth at once. "I was just going to—err, you know, I was going out. I was leaving. The house. For a bit. And then coming back. It's a great night for a walk. I mean, I figured I could leave. Now. I could leave and go for a walk. Or something like that. Now that I think about it, there's a podcast I've been meaning to listen to, and I have noise-canceling headphones. I can walk with the headphones. On my head. I won't hear anything at all. Except the podcast. I'd hear that. But you know what? I'm exhausted. Just beat. I mean—no, not that. I'm not beating anything. No. What I meant is that I'm sleepwalking. I've been told I sleepwalk. I never remember it. I don't remember anything. I won't remember any of this." I took a breath while Owen blinked at me. "This is a dream."

The tension between us jolted me back, away from the bathroom. I stumbled into the safety of my room, and shut the door behind me. I stared at the bed while my breath stuttered out in jagged bursts and my heart slammed into my ribs like it was trying to break free. My cock, unaware that this peep show had taken a turn for the incredibly awkward, was throbbing against my belly. It wasn't the kind of erection I could ignore either. I had to do something about this unless I wanted to be miserable and aching all night.

Owen's bedroom door slammed shut, and through the thin walls, I heard him moving around. I groaned again, but this time I was groaning in response to my uncanny ability to fuck things up.

As if he understood the difference, Owen chuckled. It was low and exasperated, like he couldn't believe what I'd done now.

"Sorry," I shouted at the wall.

There was another chuckle and I heard drawers opening and closing. "Go to bed, McClish," Owen replied.

Obeying this command, I stripped off my clothes and slipped between the sheets. My dick was pitching a tent that could comfortably sleep a family of four and their elderly beagle, but I forced myself to listen to the night instead of my body's drumbeat of arousal.

There were crickets and cicadas chirping in tandem and woodland creatures engaging in their nocturnal rituals. The trees rustled and the ocean lapped against the shore, and—and I heard it again. I heard *him*.

I would've missed it if not for the creaking bedsprings playing backup to his moans. Right on cue, my cock throbbed in response. I was in bad shape here. Harder than humanly possible, leaking all over the sheets, and now I had to listen while he finished the job. I was one self-indulgent second away from flopping on my belly and rutting into the mattress without concern for the current level of weird between me and Owen.

"Go to bed, Bartlett," I called.

"I *am* in bed," he shouted back. "Something's keeping me up."

I swallowed a laugh as it dawned on me. I'd announced my presence before Owen could finish, and I had to imagine he was in as much distress as I was. And I was imagining. I couldn't stop thinking about the way he touched himself. There was a frantic quality to it, as if his entire existence hinged upon finding his release.

"Sorry about that," I said.

Another garbled noise drifted through the wall from Owen's room, and my fingers found my shaft. I couldn't help it. Just couldn't help it.

"Enough apologies," he yelled.

I closed my eyes and dragged my palm up, twisting over the crown the same way Owen had. Indulging in this small dose of relief, I allowed myself to believe I was showing him what I wanted. Or it was him stroking me. Or it was my hand on his cock, and I was showing him I knew how he liked it. Then the fantasies collided, and it was all of it at once. In my mind, I gave him everything and he gave just as much in return. Cocks, hands, mouths; there was no limit.

My hips were rocking up, surging as I pumped into my hand. The motion sent the headboard knocking against the wall and the bedsprings creaking, and then I heard a very clear command from Owen. "Don't stop."

My whole body shuddered, and a grunt caught in my throat. It didn't matter whether his order was intended for me. That was how I was taking it, and I was too lost in lust to consider anything else.

"Fuck yes," I replied. I shoved my shoulders back into the mattress as I stroked harder, and the headboard hammered against the wall. "Yes, yes, *yes*."

It was a little over the top, sure. I wasn't ashamed to say there were some theatrics involved in that porn star wail. I was putting on a show, and Owen was too.

There was a thump followed by a groan that was distinctly Owen, and I could almost feel him watching me. Just as I'd watched him.

"Don't stop," he repeated, his voice rough. He sounded closer, as if he was speaking directly to the barrier between us. And there was no doubt his words were meant for me. "Don't you fucking stop."

We were no longer performing solitary acts on dueling stages, separate, and simultaneous only as a matter of coincidence. We were sharing this now.

Another thump sounded above my head, and I envisioned Owen bracing himself there as he stroked. His head would hang low, his chin resting on his chest and his eyes screwed shut as he focused on finding his release. Sweat would dot his forehead and heat would crawl up his neck and cheeks. He'd snarl and gasp as he edged closer, and slap his palm against the wall each time he denied his orgasm. Of course he'd hold back. He'd wait for me. He didn't know how to be selfish.

"Let me hear you," he rasped.

Get in here. The words were dancing on the tip of my tongue but I didn't have the backbone to say them. I couldn't disrupt the forward trajectory of this moment by requesting a left turn.

"Don't go quiet on me now," Owen said, his words huffing out in strained snarls.

"I need to come," I moan-whined.

"Maybe I'll let you," he replied.

My body was rigid with tension, every muscle held tight, and his response was a current of heat down my spine and around my cock. The challenge he levied—wait for his permission—fit like a too-tight suit, but I craved his approval more than my comfort.

"Please," I groaned, my hips jerking off the mattress as I thrust harder.

He growled, but offered nothing more.

I needed more, and I was going to get it.

I forced a breath from my lungs. My legs parted as I imagined Owen settling there, his hand gliding over his cock as he watched me. He pressed his free hand to the back of my thigh, pushing it to my chest until I was spread open for him. A feral smile tugged at his lips as he gazed at me, like he was categorizing every inch and devising methods of sexual torment. His fingers trailed down my leg and around the base of my cock. It was the lightest touch, one that seemed too gentle and measured for a man like him. But then two fingers were in my crease, then they were inside me, then I was seeing stars. Nothing gentle or measured about it.

"Oh, fuck," I sighed.

My bicep was burning and I wasn't certain I could feel some of my fingers anymore. The grip I had on my shaft was unforgiving, but I was too far down this path for any of that to matter. I was right there, teetering with little more than a toehold on my orgasm, my sanity, my consciousness.

"Owen," I gasped.

Even in this state, calling for him seemed like a step over the line. But the man between my legs, the Imaginary Finger-Fucking Owen, was nodding, granting me permission to fall over the edge.

"Give it to me now," he commanded. "Right now."

In my mind, Owen was still kneeling between my legs, the hand on his cock moving in time with the fingers in my ass. That sharp grin was still in place, and it deepened each time he traced my prostate. Instead of grinding my teeth in blissful agony, I melted into that all-the-shivers-and-goose-bumps sensation. He whispered "Mine" every time I quivered under his touch, and I nodded in agreement.

One spurt after another landed on my belly, my shoulder, the pillow. I heard a shuddering breath from Owen, and then he pounded the wall several times as he snarled and hummed. I could picture him spilling into his hand, his chest heaving and his lips parting as he growled through his release.

I was crying out and convulsing, and clinging to the quilt as if it could keep me from drifting away. But it was as though these things were happening outside of me, and I was observing them from a detached distance. Inside, I was sliding into the deep mellow of an earth-rocking orgasm. Static filled my ears and my eyelids were too heavy to lift, and every muscle in my body eased until I was nothing more than a blob of satisfied jelly.

I hated the slimy, squishy feel of semen drying on my

skin but I didn't possess the strength to clean it off. I couldn't even lift my arm and reach for a tissue from the bedside table.

Bedsprings squealed on the other side of the wall, and I knew he was tucked in for the night. A part of me—not a small part—hoped he'd trudge over here with his palm full of jizz and ask me what I planned to do about it. Hoped he'd flip me over and force me facedown on the mattress. Hoped he'd drag his thick fingers through my hair and curl up beside me.

"Good night, McClish," Owen called.

He sounded drowsy and loose, and I liked it. I wanted to get him in this state again.

"Good night, Bartlett," I replied.

A warm, sated smile tugged at my lips as I drifted off. Before sleep pulled me under, a voice in the back of my head asked, *What did we just do?*

ten

OWEN

Full and By: *adv. Sailing with all sails full and lying as near the wind as possible.*

I SLAMMED the refrigerator door shut and moved to the pantry. "Too late to make chili," I said to myself. "Too late for *good* chili."

"There's a whole haddock packed in ice," Cole called.

He was perched on the countertop, his legs hanging loose and his arms braced behind him. His skin was glowing from another sunny day on the water and his hair wind-blown. He looked like an offering, and I could only shoot quick glimpses in his direction or suffer a full-body spasm of need. Again.

I didn't know what the hell had happened last night. One minute I was lusting over athletic shorts, the next I was pressed flat against my bedroom wall and racing to keep up with Cole's strokes. Then there were his sounds and my sounds and *oh my God*. I didn't know how I was supposed to feel after masturbating with my presumably straight houseguest, so I felt a bit of everything. Excitement, anxiety, affection, amusement, shock. All of that, and a little bit of shame.

Shame wasn't an emotion I allowed myself but I couldn't think about last night without simmering in embarrassment. *How did I let it go that far? What was I thinking?* That was just it—I didn't think. Not with the head on my shoulders.

And now I'd spent the day trying to look Cole in the eye and talk about lobsters like last night was nothing more than a weird dream. Wasn't that the truth. I didn't even know this man, not really, and I was allowing myself to build these sandcastle feelings. It was dangerous, and I knew better. Summer love wasn't for me, and neither was this man. He wasn't here to stay, and he wasn't here for me. He was running away from something I didn't want to explore, but I couldn't help myself from wanting to care for him. Ease his troubles.

I snorted at that thought. His *troubles* weren't the only things I wanted to ease. I was in it with this guy, and it wasn't just me. Cole had participated too. He didn't instigate it but he certainly took an otherwise excusable situation to another level.

Even as evening settled down around us, I didn't know where I stood—*we* stood—after last night. I had an educated guess, of course. We'd shared some beers with dinner and a few more while watching the game, and liquor often blurred sexuality's not-so-tidy boxes.

Liquor was a champ when it came to taking the blame.

Not that there was much blame to go around. Jerking off with a wall between us wasn't arrow-straight, but it wasn't a subscription to the Bear of the Month club either. There was room on the rainbow for everyone.

And now I was rationalizing. Might as well explain it away before my hopes climbed all the way up and started planning some kind of future with Cole. How fucking ridiculous was that? There wasn't going to be any of that. His boat would be fixed soon enough, he'd set sail, and then I'd be right back where I always was—wondering why I'd given everything to someone who couldn't spare anything for me.

Not this time. No future, no *us*.

When I woke up this morning, hard, mortified, hungry for more, I decided I'd handle this the only way I knew how —hunkering down in my foul mood. I'd pushed Cole away with grouchy scowls and short-tempered barks all day. Avoided discussion of last night so hard I started to wonder whether it actually happened. Feigned disinterest in his chatter though I was silently soaking it all up. Busied myself with the radio, the engine, the maps—anything to keep my eyes off him. I pushed him away before he could push me.

And that approach had worked well enough while my hands were busy hauling in traps and navigating the coastline, but the sea couldn't save me now. The house seemed impossibly small, the walls and ceiling pressing in close, and I couldn't escape Cole.

Thus I was taking my sweet-ass time in the pantry. I

hoped he'd get bored soon enough and leave me in peace, but that didn't appear to be happening.

"Do you want me to get it?" he called. "The haddock?"

"Not in the mood," I called over my shoulder. "For haddock."

Important clarification. With a sigh, I pawed at a jar of preserved tomatoes from last summer, and I considered the dishes I could throw together with them. It saved me from thinking about stepping between Cole's legs and demanding his attention. I could do that. I could run my hands up his thighs, grab his waist and jerk him close. Force him to look me in the eye while my dick was pressed against his belly. Force him to account for his actions, and then beg him to give me more.

I could. I wouldn't.

"Is that allowed?" he asked. "Aren't fishermen honor-bound to eat fish all day, every day?"

"No," I said as I emerged from the pantry. "Some of us are vegetarians."

"I doubt that," Cole replied.

I did too but I enjoyed baiting him like this. Real talk—I enjoyed baiting him in all situations. Last night came to mind. But he was adorable when argumentative, all furrowed brows and aggressive gestures. Couldn't get enough of it.

He had an unshakeable belief that he was always right, and it didn't matter whether he knew anything of the topic at hand. He walked on miles-deep layers of confidence and arrogance, but I suspected I was among the lucky few to have witnessed his vulnerability too.

And then I reminded myself—once again—that he was leaving soon. He didn't have to say it. I knew. Work on his boat was coming along, and as soon as some high-tech piece of equipment came in from California, he'd set sail. I couldn't deal with the prospect of losing my new friend and the subject of my desire, and I wouldn't allow myself to ask him about it.

Avoidance, my coping mechanism of choice.

"It's true," I said. "There are entire coalitions of vegetarian fishermen—and women, of course—and they're gaining in popularity. I imagine they'll outnumber the carnivores within a decade." I gave him an earnest nod. "It will make catering at the conferences a real challenge."

Cole's forehead wrinkled as he scratched his chin. He'd taken to letting his sandy beard grow out for several days before trimming it down to scruff, and that beard had a starring role in my favorite fantasies. I'd imagined it on my neck, my chest, between my thighs. Fantasies vivid enough to wake me with an erection that seemed to throb his name.

Cole held up his hands, shaking his head. "I'm not buying it this time, Bartlett," he said. "I've gone along with one too many fish tales. I'm calling horseshit—no, *fish shit*—on this one."

"Look into it," I replied with a stiff laugh.

I set several jars and cans on the counter beside him. My fingers itched to stroke his thigh. See if it was as taut as I'd dreamed. Instead, I tossed a can of black beans from hand to hand. "Since we didn't make it to the market this morning, we're low on provisions," I said. "I can whip up—"

"Let's just go out now," he said, shrugging.

There were many things Cole still didn't understand about my world. Most notably, the closest twenty-four-hour grocery store was an hour away. "The market in town is closed," I said.

"I know that," he replied impatiently. "We'll hit the little tavern instead. It's a short walk, right? It's just through the woods. Come on, you deserve a night off from cooking. Let me take you out. My treat."

A surprised laugh bubbled up from my chest. "Are you asking me on a date, McClish?"

Cole blinked at me and then glanced away. I forced another laugh as the question went unanswered for longer than I could manage.

"I mean—" I started.

"Yeah," Cole said at the same time, a devilish grin pulling up the corners of his lips. "I'll be a perfect gentleman."

I crossed my arms over my chest and eyed him. My heart was pounding away, frantic and filled with cocksick hope. It required substantial effort to keep my expression neutral. "Couldn't if you tried."

Cole hopped off the countertop. "Now I can't let that challenge go unanswered." He glanced down at his t-shirt. "Give me a minute to make myself presentable."

"You're gonna need more than a minute," I said to his back as he walked away.

I had to curl my fingers around the edge of the countertop to restrain myself from following. I wanted, with every ounce of me, to watch him strip his clothes off. I'd sit on the edge of the bed, staring while he revealed more and more of his perfect California surfer boy skin. I couldn't imagine sitting there for long. Once he was bare, I'd drag my fingertips up his thighs, over his hips, around his backside. I'd press my chest to his back and nudge my cock between his cheeks. Make it clear what I had for him. And I had so much.

Without thinking, I thrust my hips forward, slamming hard into the cabinets. I cried out in a messy mix of pleasure and pain. The drawer handle speared into my balls, deflating my erection and driving an uncomfortable shudder through my body.

"Aw, fuck," I said, groaning. With a hand between my legs, I rubbed away the ache. I couldn't erase the fantasy behind my eyes—and the reality of it down the hall—but it helped. Closing my eyes, I pushed a breath past my lips and imagined Cole's hand caressing me.

"Hey. Are you okay, Bartlett?"

My eyes popped open and I put both hands up. "What?" I snapped, staring at him on the other side of the kitchen. "What do you want, McClish?"

"Whenever you're ready," Cole started slowly, "we can go."

"I'm ready," I replied.

I wasn't ready. I wasn't ready for any of this.

eleven

OWEN

Watching: v. When a fisherman's buoys are visible on the surface of the water due to a slack tide.

"WHAT IS the difference between baked stuffed lobster and the lazy man's lobster?" Cole asked, drumming his fingers on the tabletop. "You know, this is like ethnographic research. I should be taking notes."

"I'm sure California is dying to know all about the way real Mainers live," I replied.

"I'm sure of it," he murmured. "Foodie blog post waiting to happen." He snapped his fingers and pointed at the menu. "No vegetarian fishermen welcome here unless they're willing to settle on a side salad. Can't imagine that would satisfy you."

Cole's eyebrow arched up as he spoke and it didn't matter what he was saying because I only wanted to grab him by the neck and kiss him. All I heard was *satisfy*, and that was it.

"It's just a bowlful of chopped iceberg," I said through clenched teeth. "A slice of cucumber. Maybe a chunk of tomato."

"Like I said, that wouldn't do much for you," he replied, gesturing toward me. "You're not a side salad guy."

I met his gaze and held it for a long, challenging beat. I didn't give up so much as a blink.

"Probably not," I finally conceded. "Neither are you."

He leaned back against the booth, slowly nodding as he crossed his arms over his chest. "I see you've finally figured that out," he murmured. "Good."

What the fuck are we talking about right now? The air around us was incendiary, and nothing else existed. Not the buzzing tavern, not my issues, not his impending departure. It was just us and all the tension in the world.

And I couldn't handle it. I couldn't sit here and go round after confusing round with this guy when all I wanted was to feel his skin under mine.

"The lazy man's lobster is a regular steamed lobster, but the meat has been removed from the shell. It's lazy because you don't have to crack the shell to eat it," I said, all the words rushing out in a burst. "The baked stuffed is in the shell and stuffed with breadcrumbs." I spared him a quick glance and went back to my menu. "You'd like the swordfish. Get that."

"Would you repeat that?" he asked. "I need to write this down. I'm going to take this concept back to Silicon Valley and find someone to open a seafood restaurant with ninety-four different lobster preparations. Poke bowls are out, Maine lobster is in." He nodded several times. "I'll make a killing on it, but first you need to explain the rest of this menu to me. What in the world is a steamer?"

"It's a clam. One that's been steamed," I said. "No more questions."

"I'll hire you as my crustacean expert," he said. "Give you a cut of the profits."

"No more questions."

"I'll call it the Owen Bartlett House of Lobster," he continued.

"No, you won't."

"I will," he said. "I will and you'll be famous. Everyone will want to know the true story of this legendary lobsterman and I'll have to tell them about Talbott's Cove. You'll have reporters camped outside your house and sailing into your cove."

I rolled my eyes. "You're not supposed to threaten your date."

"You know, this isn't the first time I've received that feedback," he mused.

"Not surprising," I murmured.

Cole returned to his menu, humming and quipping as he reviewed The Galley's seemingly infinite seafood offerings, and he didn't notice Annette Cortassi approaching our booth.

Annette was sweet like maple syrup, and I believed her picture was in the dictionary right beside the entry for "girl next door." She was the best of the best people and this town was better because she was part of it, but she harbored the belief that she could flip me like a split-level house.

She was convinced we'd end up together as soon as I gave her a fair chance, and I was convinced she was delusional in that regard. I didn't think she took any specific issue with my sexuality but I was certain she saw me as subject to the power of her pussy.

The implication that I'd abandon everything I knew to be true about myself was rather insulting, but she'd learned that trick from my mother. It drove me crazy, but I chose to ignore Annette's advances. I didn't hold them against her either. No reason to make an issue out of it when I was sure she'd get the hint soon enough.

My mother was still getting the hint, but that was another issue for another day.

"Quite the pleasant surprise to see you this evening," she said when she stopped at our table. "I never see you out after sunset anymore."

Her fingertips trailed over my shoulder, and I bit back the desire to shake her off. She met my scowl with a sunny smile that glowed with real warmth, and then turned her attention to Cole.

"Is this the new deckhand I keep hearing about?"

"I prefer fishery intern," he replied, offering his hand. "Cole."

"Cole," I said, gesturing between him and Annette. "This is Annette—"

"Such a pleasure," she interrupted, taking his hand between both of hers. "It's wonderful to have you here, Cole. I hope you're enjoying your time in the Cove."

Jealousy flared hot and fast, and I wanted to snatch his hand away from her.

"Annette owns the bookstore around the corner," I said, not allowing him the time to reply.

It was rude but I didn't care. He was here with *me*. We were having dinner *together*. This wasn't an opportunity for this town's single women to rub all over my friend. My deckhand. Houseguest. Whatever the fuck he was, he was mine and not theirs.

"That I do," Annette chirped. "I can get you anything you want."

Cole leaned back against the booth as he blinked up at her. Then his eyes flicked over her body. It was quick. If I hadn't been watching, I would've missed it. I wish I'd missed it.

"Anything, huh?" he asked. "That's impressive."

"Anything at all," Annette replied. "You name it, I'll get it."

"It's funny," he started, his knuckles running along his jaw, "I can't remember the last time I read a physical book. I'm an e-book convert."

Annette offered him a patient-but-mostly-impatient smile. "There's nothing like holding a book in your hands," she said. "Maybe you could stop by some time, and we can have a little chat about your interests. I might be able to recommend something new. Something you didn't expect you'd enjoy."

I was ready to flip the table. Just lift that fucker up and throw it across the fucking room. And then I'd tell everyone listening that he was moaning in *my* ear night last night, after *I* gave him permission. It was my name he was calling when he came because he belonged to me.

I'd do it, too. I really would. I couldn't sit here and watch all these days of falling for a man who wasn't meant for me come crashing down because the town sweetheart whipped out her vagina and wielded that thing like a Venus flytrap.

"I'll keep that in mind," Cole said. His tone was pleasant, almost fond. As if he not only knew what she was implying but was actually making note of her invitation.

The hell you are.

"What about the book you're getting me?" I asked, dragging her attention away from him. "Where's my special order, Annette?"

It was such a fucked-up move. I didn't want her—of course not—but the attention she was paying Cole had me seething with jealousy.

"Oh, don't you worry, sugar," she replied, reaching out to squeeze my forearm. "It's due in next week." She tapped her chin and pursed her lips. "Come see me a week from Thursday. It should be in by then. We can take a look at the new arrivals, too. There are a few you might like. I'll set them aside. Wouldn't want anyone getting to them first." A group of women called to Annette from the bar, and she waved to them in response. "I have to get back. It's girls' night. You know how it is."

"Not really," I said flatly.

Cole caught my gaze and lifted his brows. "Not at all," he added.

Annette glanced between us and threw back her head with a hearty laugh. "You two are a hoot. Just a hoot. I love it. You must be having a whole lot of fun together," she said before aiming a manicured finger in my direction. *If you only knew, Annette. If you only knew.* "Next Thursday. I'll stay open late for you."

We watched while she retreated to her group, and I shot a glimpse across the table before turning my menu to the draft beer list. "So, that's Annette."

"Dude." Cole barked out a laugh. "She's going to *stay open late for you.*"

The implied meaning was heavy in his words.

"She has a few ideas about things." I blew out an irritable sigh. "I don't agree with all of them."

"That's not an idea, my friend. That's a heat-seeking missile." He glanced to Annette's group at the bar. Every woman was staring right at Cole—even the married ones—and if they didn't get their ovaries off him, I'd throw the fuck down. "She wants to climb you like a tree."

"There will be none of that," I murmured, shaking my head as I reread the beers. As if I didn't have this list committed to memory after a lifetime in this town.

"Yeah, I figured as much." Cole dropped his arms to the tabletop, laughing. "But she's under the impression you're bending her over a stack of books next week."

"For fuck's sake, McClish, don't you think I know?" I snapped. "That's why you're coming with me."

"You're looking to me for protection?" he asked, tapping the mint green polo shirt stretched tight across his lean chest. "I thought I wasn't allowed around knives or shotguns."

"You're not," I replied. "But I need a buffer. I haven't been alone with Annette in ten years."

He chuckled. "Based on the scene I just witnessed, she hasn't received the message you're sending."

Bringing my fingers to my forehead, I rubbed my brows until some of the frantic energy built up inside my mind dissipated. I couldn't handle all this lust, jealousy, and aggravation in one evening. I wanted to drop my head into Cole's lap and let him drag his fingers through my hair until I forgot my name. I wanted him and that want was infinitely greater than sexual desire. I wanted to fuck him straight through the summer but I also wanted to wrap my arms around him and never let go.

"I mean, she seems nice," Cole continued, "in a willfully blind sort of way. But then again, maybe she thinks you're playing hard to get. You aren't exactly an open book, my friend."

"Fuck. You're right." I whistled for the bartender's attention. "JJ," I called to him. "Double whiskey on the rocks." I glanced back at Cole and found an expectant grin on his face. I held up two fingers. "Make that two double whiskeys."

"I hate to be obvious," Cole started, "but is she aware that she isn't your type?"

"Yes." I spun the salt shaker between my palms. "I don't hide who I am."

"I wouldn't expect you to," he replied quickly. "But that only confirms my original suspicions about darling Annette."

"Which were?" I prompted.

"The bitch has balls," he said, laughing.

"No, she's..." My voice trailed off. "She's a good person.

The trouble with living in the same small town your entire life is that everyone knows your story, and everyone forms opinions of their own. And they're not alone. I know everyone else's stories, too. I have opinions about many of them." I tipped my head toward the bar. "Lincoln, the guy with the Patriots hat? I've seen him at gay bars in Portland. Often enough to know he likes the leather and Levi's scene. He's married with two kids. Then there's Fitzy, the big guy blue t-shirt? His son is going through an opioid addiction treatment program. Third time. His wife doesn't want the son back in the house after treatment on account of him stealing everything out from underneath them and selling it to buy pills. Fitzy comes here most nights to keep from arguing with her about it, and I can't say I blame him. And you've got Brooke-Ashley over there. She went to college somewhere down south, somewhere fancy and prestigious. Graduated the top of her class, found herself a big job in New York City, the whole deal. But she moved back home two years ago, and hasn't said a word about it to anyone. Some people say something terrible happened to her. Others say her father has symptoms of early-onset dementia, and she gave it all up to care for him at home." I spread my hands out in front of me. "She decided to go by Brooke when she moved away, but everyone around here still calls her Brooke-Ashley. That's how it goes in small towns."

Cole rested his elbows on the table and it required profound restraint to keep from tracing the muscular lines of his forearms. "Which opinion has Annette formed about you?"

I stared down at the salt shaker because I couldn't manage another glimpse at Annette's crew. I didn't want to get thrown out of The Galley for fighting women. "It's her position that, because I went out with a girl or two in high school, I'm not *thoroughly* gay. You know, that there's a chance I could go straight for the right woman."

JJ set two glasses on the table, making no effort to keep the liquid from sloshing over the sides. "Good luck with this," he said as he walked away.

Cole shook his head as he mopped the spilled liquor with a paper napkin. "What's with all the gold star pedants these days? My God. They're worse than the evangelicals with their concern-trolling."

"I don't know, man." With a shrug, I gulped my drink. Every ounce of that liquor was going to backhand me in the morning but I didn't care about that tonight. "But she's not the one for me."

Cole considered his glass and took a quick sip. "Good to know."

"Yeah? Why?" I asked as jealousy boiled up again. "Is she your type?"

He tipped his head to the side, a half-smile tugging at his lips. "No. I'm not into the perky-bubbly-pushy cheerleader types," he said.

"Why not?" I asked. The whiskey was already going to my head, and I could feel my words getting loose. "Everyone likes cheerleaders, with the skirts and everything."

"Not me." Cole leaned across the table, his knuckles rubbing against the back of my hand as he shifted, and he tipped his head toward me with the same half-smile he used to reject pretty cheerleaders. Every nerve in my body was pulsing at his barely there touch. "I'm not interested in women, Bartlett."

I blinked at him, frozen as he threw my exact words back at me. Every conversation, every memory of him stripping off his shirt on the boat, every sound he made last night filled my mind, and I realized this guy didn't know how to make things easy on me. He was secrets and mysteries, and one complicated mess after another. He was single-handedly ruining my quiet, comfortable existence with his questions and noise and obscene abs, and that was before I knew he was an option. Prior to this conversation, he was a short-term condition. A crush bound to end as quickly as it started.

But now—now that he'd aimed that smile at me and stroked my hand and invited me into one of his quiet truths—he was an affliction.

"Owen, say something," Cole said, his voice tinted with the same untethered panic I experienced last night. His gaze fell to the table, and he shifted his knuckles away from my hand.

"You couldn't have mentioned this earlier?"

Cole ran his hand over his jaw. "Didn't seem like the right time," he said, not meeting my eyes. "But I've wanted you since you took me home like a stray mutt."

"Yeah, I really would've appreciated this information much earlier," I said. "Last night comes to mind."

He had the decency to stare down at the tabletop while his cheeks reddened at the mention of our exchange. "You got me so hard last night," he whispered. "I needed your help."

Stunned silence didn't begin to describe my current state of existence. I could still feel his fingers on my wrist, his touch seared into my skin like a tattoo. I dragged my tongue over my parched lips. Reached for my whiskey but then put it down. Grabbed my napkin but then tossed it aside. "Sounded like you were doing just fine on your own."

"Only because I was imagining your hand on my cock," he replied. "And...elsewhere."

I locked my fingers around his wrist and tugged him back. The only words I could pull together were, "I didn't tell you to let go."

"Okay," he said, gulping. The sight of his throat bobbing turned my cock to stone. "I won't."

"Good. That's good." Without looking away from him, I called, "JJ. Another round over here."

twelve

OWEN

Harden Up: *v. To turn toward the wind; sail closer to the wind.*

"WAIT, WAIT A MINUTE," Cole hissed, his arms outstretched at odd angles as he stumbled over his feet. "Look."

I reached for the maple tree to my right, needing somewhere to lean. Leaning was easier than staying upright. "What am I looking for?"

It was late and we were drunk, but the worst part was that we'd spent the evening flirting with each other like young lovers and now I was about to explode on him. Cole knew it, too. He wanted it. The sparkle in his devious grin, the way his gaze bathed me in heat, his inability to go more than a minute without brushing his hand against mine. He wanted this as much as I did or...or he was one hell of a cockteasey drunk. God, I hoped it was the former.

"The fireflies," Cole whispered. "The louder we get, the longer they'll hide. They don't like a lot of noise or movement. Or light. But I know they're out here. Let's wait. They'll come back."

"Yeah," I replied, transferring most of my body weight to the maple. "I've seen them plenty of times." I yawned. "Is this what does it for you? Finding fireflies? You should've told me that two weeks ago."

Cole crouched down low, and he was quiet for a long moment. "I went to Tennessee once. There's a researcher there, an old woman who specializes in the Smoky Mountain Synchronous Firefly." He stood, turning in a small circle. "*Photinus carolinus*," he added, as if I required that detail. "The males, they flash in a synchronized rhythm. It's a mating call. But they only live in certain regions."

"Like, the Smoky Mountains?" I asked around a laugh.

"Well, yes," he replied. "And a few other regions in southern Appalachia."

"Can't picture you in southern Appalachia," I murmured. Cole was too busy tracking fireflies to hear.

"I brought a group of my—uh—businesspeople to the Appalachian Trail," he continued. "I had this big idea about sparking some childlike wonder and nostalgia for the ways things used to be. You know, summer camping trips. The great outdoors."

"And fireflies," I offered.

"And fireflies," he repeated. He gestured for me to follow him. I reluctantly pushed away from the tree, but the motion sent me colliding with his shoulder. His arms went around me, his palms settling on my belly and the small of my back to keep me steady. "Easy there, big guy."

"I'm good, I'm good," I said, righting myself. But my

body was aglow where he'd touched me. I patted his shoulder—a gesture of thanks—but lingered a couple of seconds too long. Not long enough.

"Some species of firefly are dying out," Cole said. Apparently he didn't require full minutes to process my touch before forming words. Lucky Cole. "Skyglow, the phenomenon of constant brightness from cities, highways, and screens, interferes with their ecosystems. And I took a bunch of businesspeople—the kind who built their careers on technological advancement—into the Smoky Mountains to catch a look at some fireflies."

"Did that work out as intended?"

"Not at all," Cole said, laughing. "The researcher, she wouldn't allow us to bring any phones or tablets—like I said, screens are part of the problem—or flashlights."

His words hitched as he stumbled over an exposed tree root in the path. I dropped my hand onto his shoulder again, and kept it there this time.

For safety. Of course.

"There'd been a forest fire the previous season, and some of the trails were gone. We didn't get lost because this researcher knew the forest like the back of her hand, but the journey didn't go as planned. We didn't get to see any fireflies, not really. There was some twinkling in the distance, but the fire did a number on their population." He sighed, and I squeezed his shoulder in response. "They missed the point I was trying to make."

"You're getting some fireflies now," I whispered.

Cole didn't respond. He was staring into the woods,

pointing and murmuring in delight as he spotted another zip of light.

"It really is something when you think about it," he said. "Adult fireflies are only active for about two weeks. They live for almost two years but they spend most of that time eating bugs and hanging around, not doing much of anything. Just waiting and waiting for that snap of time when they have to find a mate, and then they only have two weeks to get the job done."

"Seems like a lot of pressure," I said.

"But isn't that the way? You spend forever waiting for the right time, but then the right time is over before you know it." Cole shrugged, and I gulped down a groan at the feel of his muscles rising and falling beneath my touch. "That's probably why they have extremely active sex lives."

"Someone should have an extremely active sex life," I muttered.

"Once they find a mate, it takes almost an hour to transfer the sperm," Cole said. It sounded like he was reading from a textbook. A sexy textbook about horny fireflies. Or something.

"Sounds good to me."

"Once it's done, the sperm transfer, the male stays around to ward off competitors. He doesn't want anyone else getting in there." He shrugged again, and if I was sober, I'd think he rubbed his cheek against my hand. Then again, if I was sober, I wouldn't be massaging his shoulder in the woods at night. I would've moved this conversation somewhere with beds. And lube. "They're territorial fuckers."

"Me too," I said. Not sober, not sorry.

Cole stopped, and pointed toward the woods. It was dark back here, completely hidden from the lighthouse's steady beacon, and that darkness awakened a whirl and flow of tiny stars. They blinked in the quiet beat of an ancient universe to which we were guests, voyeurs in a mating ritual that mirrored my own wants.

"I get it," I said slowly. "The nostalgia. It feels pure. Or, as pure as any booty call can be."

"That wasn't what I wanted my team to walk away with, but it's true," Cole replied. "I wanted them to think micro—the fireflies—and macro—us—but they weren't picking up on any of that."

He sighed and this time he definitely rubbed his cheek on my hand. That scruff. *Ah.*

"They're flashing us their happy little dick pics," Cole said. "This is just a whole lot of dick announcing *I'm down to fuck*."

"We're basically watching a glow-worm orgy," I said.

"I know," he whispered. "It's awesome until you really think about it."

"You should've told that team of yours about the sex. That got my attention."

"Should we give them some privacy?" Cole asked.

I started to respond but instead of speaking, I pressed my lips to his neck. My hand moved from his shoulder to his chest, and I dragged him closer to me. I should've stopped. Should've pushed him away, put this on hold, and figured out what the fuck we were doing because the heat between us was increasing by the second and I was a breath away from losing my thoughts—every one of my damn thoughts—and letting need guide the way. But I didn't do that.

For once in my life—twice, if we were counting last night's indiscretions—I did what I wanted rather than thinking about the implications and repercussions. I brought my hand to Cole's face, turned him away from the glow-worm orgy, and kissed him.

In the back of mind, I knew...one wrong move and this could end with some awkward moments and hard feelings, and I didn't want either for us. He was an unexpected friend, and one I wasn't ready to lose.

He twisted in my arms, his lips returning to mine, his hands shifting down to my waist, his knuckles stroking the small of my back in the most precious way, and I fell over the edge of reason. It was like those seconds between barreling over the bow and splashing down in the ocean, when all sense of balance and equilibrium went wild before recalibrating as the water took over.

I cupped his face and pressed my lips to his in a kiss that was too tortured, too desperate to be the kind of kiss he deserved. We clawed at each other, pushing and pulling and grabbing in a battle for touch that would have no end.

"Tell me we're doing this," he panted against my lips.

"What is *this*?" I asked. I needed him to spell it out. Draw the map and show me the course. There could be no miscommunication here. "What do you want?"

Cole pressed his face to the crook of my neck, his lips exploring my skin as his hand traveled down until it squeezed my cock. It was exactly as firm and confident as

I'd imagined last night. Before I found him outside the bathroom, and after.

"I want this," he said, releasing a hot breath on my neck.

Grabbing his shoulders, I pushed him back far enough to catch his eyes. My touch was rough, nearly punishing, and I would have regretted that if it weren't for the blissed-out sigh on Cole's lips.

Yesssss.

"Say it," I ordered, my hold on him tightening.

"I want you. So much that it hurts," he said, his words tumbling out in a gasp.

There was only one way to ease this pain. Without a word, I backed him up against a tree and dropped to my knees. My hands were curled around his hips while I pressed my face to his heat. He was thick and hard behind his shorts, and I dragged my scruffy chin over the fabric to feel the length of him.

"Do that one more time and I'm gonna come in my pants," Cole said, his words slurring around a hiccup.

"Are you too drunk for this?" I asked. I was unbuttoning his shorts while I asked, but I still asked. "I don't want you to regret this tomorrow."

Cole shook his head but it had the effect of shaking his entire body. I had to lash my arms around his waist to keep him from hitting the ground. "Nope," he drawled. "I'm a sloppy drinker. It's my worst trait. That, and my penchant for screaming at the people who work for me. But anyway. No, I'm completely lucid under this. I can't turn it off. I've tried. Once, in college, I tried to get drunk enough to find women attractive. Like, sexually. I mean, women are beautiful but—"

"Is there a point?"

I shoved his boxer briefs down and his cock swung free. It tapped my cheek, and though I wanted more than anything to get my hands on him, I waited. I didn't know where that Herculean strength sprang from, but I appreciated the hell out of it now.

"Yes, there's a point, Owen," he replied, exaggerating every word like a sassy teenager. "It's that there's nothing I can do to turn off my mind. That's the trouble with having an extremely high IQ. It's one of the highest ever recorded."

"Don't make me gag you," I said, then thought better of it. "Unless you'd like that."

"No, I wouldn't," he said. "But if you don't suck my dick right now, I'm gonna think you don't know how to."

I shook my head but took pity on him, wrapping my fingers around his shaft before brushing my lips over the crown. He was thick and warm, and he smelled like the most hedonistic heaven I could imagine. "Always something to say."

Cole's hands landed on my shoulders, and he gripped me hard. "Do that again," he ordered.

I thought about teasing him. If this was a random hookup, I would've. I usually answered demands with more torment. Same with pleading and begging. But rather than wanting to assert my control, I wanted to give Cole what he needed. Even if that meant ceding some of that control.

"Please, again," he begged.

"Anything," I whispered, laving my tongue over him. I learned the contours of him, licking up and down his length, around his crown. It didn't take long—maybe a minute or two—but for me it was an epic journey. I was Magellan here, and I was intent on mapping my new world.

Cole's hands slipped up my neck and into my hair, his hips pumping as I worked him. The woods seemed to close in, the night joining forces with the noises of nature and the raw smell of earth to surround us. It was primal, as if the woods were calling on me to make this man mine.

The cloak of darkness offered a voyeuristic sanctuary, a secret as long as we didn't mind the audience. The damp soil beneath my knees, the lightning bugs and beetles fluttering around us, the creatures lurking in the distance, the whisper of trees and the roar of the sea—it all rose up like an unblinking chorus.

I swallowed him down, inch by inch, and sighed in delight when my nose brushed against his pelvis. His scent was different here, richer. In the back of my mind, I knew I'd never be able to venture into these woods without recalling his scent. I wasn't prepared to deal with that thought or the possibility that this man could mean something—maybe everything—to me, and shoved it far away while I worked on showing off the best of my blow job skills.

And when it came to skills, I had them. No one racked up a decade's worth of meaningless sexual encounters without learning their way around a topflight blow job.

Cole's fingers tightened around my hair. "I'm," he

started, his voice pitching high while my fist moved him fast and my tongue rolled along the underside of cock. His back arched away from the tree. "I'm—*mmm*—yes."

I hummed in response and dragged my free hand away from his hip and between his legs. My touch was light and gentle as my fingertips ran up his thigh, over his sac, and between his crease. I was as surprised as anyone that I could not only manage light and gentle but enjoy it, too.

I was good at rough, hard, fast, and I guess that fit. I was a big guy who worked on lobster boats. Of course I'd fuck as rough and hard as I worked. But—no. No, that didn't fit. A man possessed more facets than his profession, and I knew that to be true because I wanted to lay Cole on my bed, massage every inch of his body, and take him as soft and sweet as he could bear. And then I wanted him to do the same to me.

"Ohhh."

I glanced up and found Cole's head tilted back against the tree, his eyes screwed shut and his chest heaving. Even in the darkness I could make out a rosy flush across his sharp cheekbones. I wanted to tell him he was beautiful and goofy and erotic, all at once. I wanted to watch the way my words affected him. I wanted him to give me his words, and I wanted them to come from the same confusing places as mine.

But I didn't. I went on sucking him, stroking him, speaking my desires the only way I knew how. This night offered no place for my heart and its flowery notions, and I could live with that as long as I could spend it with Cole in my arms.

I pushed a finger inside him and he cried out, a sound that was at once desperate and vicious. His balls were tight and heavy against my wrist, and I doubled down on my efforts, swallowing him deep while I massaged that magical spot.

"What the fuck are you doing to me? What the running fuck is happening right now?" Cole hissed. "This is what a supernova feels like. Or breaking the sound barrier. Or cold fusion. Maybe dark matter. I don't know much about that but—"

He didn't finish that thought because he popped off like a shot down my throat. He went on sighing and groaning as I licked every drop and then mapped his skin with my lips. Minutes passed while he fought to catch his breath, his fingers still tight around the strands of my hair.

My cock was throbbing to the point of pain. It was like one of those old cartoons where a character knocked himself in the head with a hammer, and the resulting goose egg pulsed white to red, white to red. A snarl was building in my throat and I was ready to pounce. Tear his clothes, spin him around, bend him over, take what I wanted. Needed.

As much as my body wanted that, my heart didn't. Regardless of whether I'd recently blown his mind, I couldn't bring myself to unleash that kind of self-serving desire on him. It was silly, really. This was a summer fling at best; a one-night stand at worst. He was leaving and I was staying, and there was no sense winding myself up with emotional ideas. But I was already wound up, long past silly, on my way to lovesick.

Cole's grip on my hair loosened. "I hope you're not done with me."

I kissed the jut of his hipbone and shook my head, stealing another lungful of his scent. "Not even close," I replied.

Cole blew out a breath as a growl rattled in his throat. He dragged his fingers over my scalp and canted my head to meet his hungry gaze. His eyes were hooded but sober as a sermon. He tipped his chin down. "Zip me up."

Taking orders wasn't my style but serving Cole was. I'd been serving him since the minute he'd drifted into my cove, and I wasn't about to stop.

"A 'please' wouldn't be too hard, would it?" I asked, dragging my teeth over the same hipbone I'd adored seconds ago. "Or am I just someone to put your dick away for you, little prince?"

Cole fisted my hair, snickering. "I've said it about nine thousand times tonight."

I sucked a mark into his skin and then pulled his boxer briefs up, careful to snap the waistband when they were in place. "If you know what's good for you, you'll keep saying it," I murmured. "You can be bossy or bratty, but not both."

"I think you like both."

His shorts were in a heap around his ankles, and I did my best to shake the dirt and forest miscellany from them before sliding them up his lean legs. "You don't know what I like."

Cole wrapped his hand around my bicep and hauled me up from the ground. "I'm gonna find out." He busied himself with pinching the seams of my t-shirt and straightening my clothes. He ran his hands from my shoulders to my fingertips, and then pressed his palm to my aching cock. "Real soon."

All the strength in the world couldn't keep me from whispering, "Please."

thirteen

COLE

Harden In: *v. To haul in the sheet and tighten the sails.*

THERE WERE steps between that spot in the woods and Owen's bedroom, many of them, but he took my hand and guided me down the path, and everything else drifted away. I wanted to take a picture of us, just like this. My man, holding my hand as he led the way. *My man.* Now, that was a rare thought.

Once we were behind closed doors, he attacked my clothes. Unbuckle, unzip, unbutton, off. When my boxers hit the floor, Owen stepped back and stared at me, drinking in my bare skin.

Before modesty could get the better of me, I gripped my cock at the base and gave it a lazy stroke. A growl rumbled up from his chest and his brows lowered in warning. His breath was coming in quick, rough pants that worked me like a seductive lullaby. I knew nothing beyond hunger, absolute starvation for this man.

"Off," I said, reaching for his t-shirt.

"Now you're thinking," he replied. "Thought you were just going to make me watch while you jerked it. Not that I'd complain but that wasn't what I had in mind."

I yanked the shirt up and over his head, and then moved on to his shorts but I was a disaster. At least one button was sacrificed to the cause and I gave up trying to maneuver the zipper around the substantial bulge of his erection. Bypassing the zipper altogether, I dragged the garment down his hips and sighed in relief when he was free of it.

"Shit. Sorry about that," I mumbled. "I'm not great in the dark. Or with undressing. That's not what I meant. No, I mean, obviously I know how to get undressed. I'm just not experienced when it comes to taking off someone else's clothes. It's not one of my skills. I might be a born-again virgin."

Owen—God love him—chose that moment to cross his arms over his thick chest.

"You say that like it's a bad thing. It's not. I'll teach you anything you need to learn," he said, his dick pointing straight at me. He reached out, his knuckles skimming down the line of my jaw. "You did just fine, little prince."

I didn't know what it was about his acceptance and affection, but it gave me wings. I wasted no time backing him to the bed, flattening him against the quilt, and taking his cock in my mouth. I couldn't remember the last time I'd sucked someone off but what I lacked in talent, I made up for in enthusiasm. I was eager to have this—and him—and

I packed years of need and loneliness, desire and relief, into every roll of my tongue.

I sucked him deep and hard, and his hands were everywhere. Tight around my shoulders. Rubbing my scalp. Stroking my jaw. And then his hand found mine. Our fingers laced together, our eyes met. Seeing him there, his eyes narrowed as I brought him to the edge, his hips rolling against the bed as he fucked my mouth, it turned me on like nothing else.

And it had Owen erupting like a geyser.

"You taste like the ocean," I murmured after I'd swallowed every pulsing spurt. "I liked it."

"That's the right answer," Owen said, a sated laugh ringing in his words. His hand was on my shoulder and he squeezed, pulling me closer. "Come here. I want to play with you a little before I fuck you."

I peered up at him from between his thick thighs. "What?"

"Is that all right?" he asked, edging up on an elbow. "Or do you need to take a break?

"No." I was kneeling at his feet, my arms around his waist and my cheek pillowed on the warm skin above his knee where his tan and freckles faded away. He smelled like sex and dirt, and it was the truest moment I'd ever lived. This was the only place I wanted to be. If I closed my eyes and concentrated on the thrum of his pulse under my ear, I could keep this. "No," I repeated.

Owen sat up, his brows furrowing as he moved. "No, it's not all right?" he asked, his fingers rubbing the back of my neck. "Or no, you don't need a break?"

I tilted my head to get a better look at him. "What? I didn't catch any of that."

He hummed to himself and pushed his fingers through my hair. "Are you sure you're not too drunk for this?"

I shook my head. "Not drunk at all. Not anymore."

Owen hooked his arm around my torso and hauled me onto the bed. "That helps, I suppose."

I sat beside him and rested my head on his shoulder. "I'm just a little—I don't know. Dazed?"

"Dick drunk?" he offered.

"Probably, yes." I laughed, and waved toward his crotch. "How could I not be? With all that?"

"I'm glad you enjoyed it," he said, laughing. He kissed my forehead and dropped his hand onto my chest, pushing me back. "Get on your belly. I want to spend some time with your ass."

That was all I needed to hear. It was *everything* I needed to hear. I crawled to the middle of the bed, my skin burning under the heat of Owen's gaze. His fingertips brushed over the back of my calf and up my leg. A shiver started at my shoulders and moved through my body.

"Something you like?" Owen asked.

One finger traced the seam of my knee. His touch was barely there but the anticipation only doubled the impact. "Mmhmm," I murmured against the quilt. The rhythm was slow but purposeful. He wanted me to know how he'd tease me elsewhere.

The mattress dipped at my waist. He planted his hand near my shoulder, brushed his lips over my neck. "Then I'll keep going," he said, his breath warm on my skin.

I shivered again. "Please."

Owen dragged his lips down my spine, licking and kissing as he passed each notch. "You're fucking golden," he whispered.

"And you like that?" I asked. "That I'm golden?"

I felt him nod, his scruff scraping over the tender part of my flank. Goose bumps rippled over my skin. "Love it," he murmured. "I've always wanted my very own California boy."

For the first time, I glanced back at him. He didn't notice. His cock was jutting out from his body. He was thick and throbbing, the head shiny with a dot of arousal. "I can't believe you're hard again," I said.

"Why not? Haven't you seen yourself?"

He moved to my waist, his hands locked around my hips, and hiked me up. His palms smoothed down my back and over my ass, his thumbs sliding between my crease with enough pressure to have my breath shuddering out.

"Not from that angle," I replied.

"It's a good angle." Owen laughed as he squeezed my backside, each finger triggering a rush of need like cracks in a dam. "Then again, you're hot from every angle."

His grip tightened and then—*oh, fuck*—his tongue swiped over my flesh. "Oh, my God."

A growl was the only response I received. He went on tormenting me while I clawed the quilt down and flung pillows to the floor. It was all I could do.

"This ass is so sweet," Owen said. He reached between my legs, gripped my shaft. "I'm gonna tear it up."

His fingers moved down my cock with quick, light

strokes. It wasn't enough, and he knew it. He chuckled as I thrust into his fist, trying and failing to find more friction.

"Now, please," I said.

"This," he said, his thumb stroking the head as he kissed up my spine, "*this* is what I was thinking about last night. You, on my bed. Naked. Panting. Pleading."

"Did you think about fucking me at any point?" I asked. "Because that would be great right now."

Owen laughed. "Yeah, I thought about that all night." He patted the mattress around me, searching until his fingers closed around the condom packet. I heard the rip, then the glug of lube into his palm, then the rasp of his short beard on my lower back. "Ready?"

"Very." I squirmed, desperate to feel him inside me. "Don't tease me, Owen. I can't, I—" The words caught in my throat as he pushed into me. He felt like iron, hard and unyielding. My body burned, vulnerable and hot as I forced myself to breathe through the stretch and sting.

"If you think I have the strength to tease you, you haven't been paying attention," Owen said. "If anyone's the tease here, it's you."

He rested both hands on my waist, his thumbs massaging my lower back while he inched inside me. Every thrust drew a gasp from my mouth and then a quiet prayer for more. He leaned down when he was fully seated, and brushed his lips over the base of my neck.

Tears sprang to my eyes, not from pain but the emotional impact of opening myself to a man for the first time in years. As if he was dragged under the same overwhelming wave, Owen kissed my neck and shoulders.

"Okay?" he asked, his hips moving faster now. "Is this good?"

"Yes great please more don't stop," I begged.

He kissed me again, and then I sensed him pulling away. "Good," he said.

The heel of his palm pressed the base of my neck, his fingers sliding, fisting in my hair. He had me anchored there, my cheek flat on the mattress and the sheets balled in my hands. My lips were parted on an infinite moan as he pounded me.

He was going at me hard, there was no doubt about that, but it was perfect. I didn't know it when I set out on this summer journey, but I needed this. Not a fling, not a rough hookup, but Owen. I needed him to dirty me up, take me apart.

Reaching around, Owen took my length in hand. "I'm there," he said, his words nothing more than a groan. "Need you there, too."

I couldn't put thoughts together right now. All I could manage was a murmur and a nod, and a hard thrust onto his cock. I was full beyond belief, every inch of my skin electrified with sensation.

"For a born-again virgin, you know how to work that ass. Show me," he ordered. "Show me how you like it, baby."

My eyes were barely open, my lips parted, my body slick with sweat. I brought my hand to my erection, wrapping my fingers around Owen's, and showed him what I wanted. "This," I said, the word muffled against the mattress. "Just like—"

The pressure of our hands, his cock, his body over mine, it hit me at once. I fell apart, came back together, and then fell all over again. I heard him roar and pant, I heard him yell my name like no man had ever yelled it before, and I felt his body go slack against mine. He ran his hands over me, rubbing and squeezing me as he went. I couldn't manage more than the occasional moan or sigh, and I hoped the sloppy, sated grin on my face said it all.

"I'll be right back," Owen said, his lips pressed beneath my ear. "You stay right here."

"Don't think I can move," I mumbled.

The mattress shifted as he rolled away from me. Then, the floor creaked under his feet, a sudden reminder that I wasn't actually floating on a cloud of warm marshmallows but in this man's seaside cottage, sweaty and used in the best way. And I knew—once again—that I didn't want to be anywhere else.

Owen returned a few minutes later, a damp cloth in hand. He cleaned me up and fixed the bedding, all while I smiled up at him.

"You look like a Renaissance painting," he said, tossing a pillow at my head. "A slutty Renaissance painting."

"The best kind," I said.

He tugged the sheets up to my waist and slipped in behind me. He said nothing. I wanted him to respond, tell me he liked it when I was a little slutty. I wanted some recognition that he enjoyed teasing me as much as I enjoyed teasing him. I wanted something, anything to confirm that we hadn't made a huge mistake.

"Are you all right?" Owen asked, his hand skimming down my flank.

"I'm good," I said. "This was good."

Owen started to say something but stopped himself. I need him to say something. Eventually, he curled his arm around my waist and blew out a breath. "Get some rest, McClish. The sun's up in a few hours."

It wasn't what I needed, but it was something.

fourteen
COLE

Above Board: *n. On or above the deck; in plain view; not hiding anything.*

OWEN WAS AWAKE FIRST. I didn't have to look outside to know he was on the dock, readying the *Sweet Carolyne*, because recent days had taught me he was a creature of habit. A habit that excused him from acknowledging that we'd spent the night curled around each other. It was simpler this way. Simple was good, at least for today.

But as the dawn broke into day, I was increasingly confused about where things stood. It wasn't like Owen was the kind of guy who enjoyed sitting down for tea and sorting it all out. That was another place where we deviated. My brain preferred the precise, and without it, I was edgy and untethered. Aside from the tug of my sore, satisfied muscles, it was an ordinary outing on the water followed by a trip to the local market, and dinner on the porch, and the entire time, I wanted to scream, "*What is going on with us?*"

Of course I didn't. I'd made it to thirty-four years old without experiencing a relationship of any substance. Dating in Silicon Valley was fraught with complications. People were drawn to me for my money, my status, my power, but never once for *me*. On most days, I doubted that anyone in the Valley knew me at all. Sure, I was the CEO—err, former CEO—with the temper and the track record of transforming the industry, but that wasn't the sum of my parts.

But Owen...he didn't know the CEO. He didn't know any of it, and in that, he was the only one who knew me.

And that was what made the possibility of Owen telling me it was a one-night thing the worst scenario. That he didn't want more, or didn't want more of *me*, and it would be finished for us.

Instead of talking through my issues, I'd skipped the preseason NFL game and retired to the guest room to work on some programming projects after dinner. It was an out for Owen. If he didn't want anything more than a deckhand, I wasn't going to force the issue.

My phone blew up with notifications every time I powered it on, but I ignored all of them tonight. Neera's messages were the only ones that interested me. That, and I required a distraction.

Neera: People are starting to ask questions about your vacation. I don't have anything to tell them.

Cole: Are they wondering if it's permanent?
Neera: Some, but not all. A few questions about whether you're working for the government. A few questions about whether you're working against the government. Others have asked if you're writing a book, starting a new company, in rehab, planning a run for office.
Neera: It's mostly BS. Not difficult to shut down.
Cole: Good.
Neera: It would be easier if I had the real story and didn't look as clueless as everyone else. You know the bloggers and reporters come to me before going to the PR team.
Cole: You know what they say about secrets.
Neera: Three people can keep them so long as two are dead.
Cole: There you go.

BUT THEN, not long after I'd opened my laptop and dived into coding headspace, Owen barged into the room wearing only his boxer briefs. I blinked twice as I dragged my glasses down my nose because *holy fuck*, that man was beautiful. He was a bear. A big, angry bear.

He beckoned me toward him with a hot stare. "Why aren't you in bed?"

I ran my hand over the quilt beneath me in what I hoped to be an illustrative response.

"My bed," he clarified.

"*Your* bed?" I repeated. "You mean—"

"Get your ass in there right now," he barked. "What are you even doing in here?"

I gestured to my laptop. Did he want to know the

specifics of the program I was developing? That didn't seem likely. Owen was one of a dying breed that lived happily without the quicksand of the internet. He preferred walking inside the bank to speak with a teller when making a transaction. He relied on maps and tide charts rather than modern—and surprisingly finicky—navigation systems. He even had an old-fashioned rotary phone on the kitchen wall. Before I'd arrived, there was no internet access in his home. I'd fixed that, of course, but I wasn't troubling him with those details.

"Working," I said, and I hoped it didn't sound overly evasive.

A sound rumbled in his throat that sent shockwaves through my body. "I meant," he started, rubbing the back of his neck, "why the fuck are you working in *here*? Why aren't you next door?"

My eyes darted to the screen for a moment, hoping to find the words between the lines of code. I could offer an excuse about needing quiet or my gear but knowing that he wanted me again—that he wanted me *at all*—changed things. It gave me a bite of confidence I'd never known I was lacking.

"I didn't know you wanted that," I said.

Owen cocked his head, squinting at me. "Was there something vague about my dick in your ass this morning?"

Gulp. I could still feel his weight on me, his hands on my hips, my groans into the mattress.

"But—but—you didn't say anything. You haven't said anything all day. I've had no idea what you want and what you're thinking," I said. "For all I know, it was a one-and-done thing for you."

"More like four," he quipped.

"What?" I asked, shaking my head.

"I meant," he started, "last night was more like four-and-done."

I ran my hand through my hair. "I didn't know you'd want that again."

"Do you?" he asked, his gaze darting away from mine.

"Yes," I answered. "If you do."

"Okay." He nodded decisively. "Good."

"Yeah, it's great that it's good and all, but this has been really confusing," I said, my voice raising. "You could've given me—I don't know—any indication of what you were thinking as to prevent me from creating insane scenarios in my head."

"Is that what you need?" Owen asked. His words were slow and soft, like he'd wrapped them in a blanket especially for me. "Me talking about things?"

"Yeah. I need you to tell me what's going on, even if it's nothing. I need you to be up front with me."

I bobbed my head in an effort to force back the reminder that I wasn't giving Owen any of the things I demanded. He didn't know the truth about me, and I should've told him sometime before my cock met the back of his throat.

"It's not nothing," he growled. "How could this be nothing?"

I looked back to the screen, the one place I always knew what to do and how to communicate, but before I could formulate a response, Owen was wedging himself beside me on the bed.

"Put this thing away," he said, his voice husky in my ear.

I obeyed. Of course I did. How could I do anything but exactly what Owen wanted when his lips were ghosting over my neck and shoulders?

His big hand settled on my chest and tugged my shirt up, over my head. He drew his knuckles down the centerline of my abs and dipped just below the waistband of my shorts. His fingers didn't move any farther down, instead stroking the fine trail of hair and stirring me to life.

"Did I not take care of you, my little prince?" Owen asked.

I'd never found myself on the receiving end of a pet name before, and I'd never imagined I'd like it. But I did. I liked it a lot.

Open-mouthed kisses covered my chest, and I felt myself unraveling like a tightly bound spool of thread. My head dropped back to the pillow, my legs parted, and all the weight I'd been carrying in my chest transformed into desire.

"Ah, no, you...you're amazing," I said, my eyes closing as his tongue found my nipple. "But it's complicated for me. There are a few things we should talk about."

I didn't want to withhold the truth any longer. He deserved to know that I wasn't just me, but me plus a worldwide empire, a mind-boggling fortune, and an entire blogosphere dedicated to reporting on my every eyebrow twitch.

Owen shook his head against my belly. "You're thinking too hard," he said, dropping kisses up my torso. "But you're probably right. I'll go first, and I won't tease you while I do it." He sat up and folded his hands in his lap.

"But I enjoyed the teasing," I complained. "Please, tease away."

"After," he promised. "I had a physical in June, and my blood work checks out. I haven't been with anyone since then, but I understand if you want to use condoms anyway."

"Oh, yeah," I said, reminding myself that normal people had conversations like this when they were sleeping together. "I'm good, too, on the health stuff."

"And you prefer bottoming?" he prompted. "Or did I read that wrong?"

"No, you're right," I said, swallowing a lusty sigh. I didn't know how I was going to pivot this discussion.

"Have you ever topped?"

"Yeah." I jerked a shoulder. "A long time ago. College. Not since."

"Would you do it again?" Owen asked. "If I asked you?"

I watched while he traced the line of hair running down my chest and past my belly button. "You'd want that? With me?"

"That's the second time tonight you've questioned my interest in you," he said, his gaze trained on my skin. "I can't decide whether you can't see yourself with a guy like me or you don't realize you're one helluva catch."

I ran my finger over the crease in his forehead. "What do you mean by that? A guy like you?"

"You know what I mean."

Owen glanced up from the spot he'd claimed on my abs and met my gaze with an arched eyebrow. Our backgrounds weren't the same, I knew that. But if he wanted to make something about the differences between us—economic, social, geographic—he was going to have to use his words and tell me that. I wasn't going to accept any assumptions on the matter, not when I believed these differences were exceedingly manageable. We'd made it this far without finding ourselves tangled in a different world knot. Why make one now?

When I shook my head, he blew out an impatient breath. "Dammit, McClish. A guy who wants you to fuck him. All right?" He rubbed his lips along the waistband of my boxers. "I'm just a guy who wants your cock. Can you live with that? Can you find it in yourself to bend me over and nail me one of these days?"

"Yeah, I can live with that," I replied with a snort. "Just let me know when you want to get nailed."

A grin pulled at the corner of his mouth. "I will," Owen promised. He scooted down, between my legs, and pressed his face to my crotch. He nuzzled my cock, his chin and lips stroking me through my boxers. The friction was unreal. When his hand slipped under my hip to nudge my back channel, I almost sprang off the bed.

That was all I could take. My cock was hard, my skin tight and hot, and I was nearly cross-eyed with need but I didn't want to be deceptive. It wasn't right, and Owen deserved to know who he was fucking.

"I want you right now," I whispered, "but we should talk first."

"We've done enough talking," he said, his fingers hooking around my shorts. "I've wanted you since you tried to shoot me off your boat, and if you didn't know it then, you knew it when you started whipping your shirt off in front of me every afternoon. End of discussion."

He shifted to slip out of his boxer briefs, and the motion sent his thick cock slapping against his belly. I reached forward, hungry for it—for *him*—and led him down with a firm grasp on his length.

"It's hot out there," I murmured, dropping a kiss on the corner of Owen's mouth.

He gave me *don't I know it* eyes. "*You're* hot out there."

He reached between my legs and trailed his fingers along my crease. I'd surrender everything in the known world to feel him there, more gentle than any man his size had a right to be, for the rest of my life. And it wasn't just his touch. It was his everything.

"I need," I said, groaning when Owen's fingers pressed between my cheeks as he took me in his mouth. All the fucks, *yes*. My eyes drooped shut, and stars and rainbows danced behind my lids. "We need to get the lube from your room. You're too big for me without it."

He looked up, confused. That had the unfortunate effect of separating his mouth from my erection.

"You don't have any?" Owen asked.

I shook my head as a whiny groan rattled in my throat. My hips jerked upward, seeking his attention. I was shameless when it came to him.

"We need to work on your preparedness," he said.

I looked away, not sure how to respond to him. "I didn't expect to get laid this summer," I confessed. "That wasn't even on my short list of priorities."

Owen brought his palms to his thighs with a decisive nod. "Well, you're getting laid tonight. Tomorrow night, too. Then there's next week, and the week after that. If you're up for it, of course. If Maine is on your short list of priorities."

I needed this, for as long as I could get it. I'd give up everything if it meant more time with Owen. I sat up on my knees and roped my arms around his waist. "It's my only priority."

Owen's gaze darkened as he stared at my mouth. His palm cracked over my ass, and as I yelped in surprise, he said, "Go get in *our* bed."

I'd never chased after a man before, but when Owen marched down the hall, his erection slapping against his belly loud and proud, I wasn't ashamed to say I power-walked myself right after him.

"Get comfortable," Owen ordered, pointing to the bed. He was digging in a bureau drawer, his back to me. I turned down the blankets and slipped between the sheets, but I couldn't tear my eyes off his body. His shoulders were like a mountain range.

"What are you doing?" I whined. I was losing my mind watching him like this, the muscles in his ass flexing every time he shifted on his feet. It was like watching two puppies wrestling under a blanket. My legs parted and my hand went to my erection. I needed some relief.

"Looking for the good lube," he replied. "I figure you're worth it."

I kicked the sheets off. Too hot, too much. "You better believe I'm worth it."

"This drawer is a mess," Owen grumbled. "I can't believe I let it get this bad."

"I can't believe you're talking about messy drawers right now," I complained. "I *am* naked."

Owen shifted, his eyes glazing over when he caught sight of me in the center of his bed, cock in hand. "That you are," he murmured. "And what a sight you are, my little prince."

I blinked, and then I noticed it. In one hand, Owen held three dildos. In the other, two metal butt plugs of differing sizes. "Umm. What the hell are we doing with all that?" I asked.

He glanced down at his hands, his eyes widening as he assessed the toys. "Nothing," he replied with a laugh. He dumped them back in the drawer and then slammed it shut. "We'll play with those some other time."

I gulped. "We will?"

"If you want." Owen yanked open the top drawer on the bedside table. "There it is," he said to himself. He tossed a bottle of lube to the bed and climbed up beside me. "I really need to organize this stuff."

"You have a lot of toys," I said, dragging my fingertips down his chest. "*A lot* of toys."

"Does that interest you?" He smiled when I nodded in response. "Good. Now, get your hands off that dick. It's mine."

Owen nestled between my legs and pushed my thighs back. I watched while he poured lube into his palm, and slicked his fingers and my crease. Cool liquid between my legs had me tensing back a shiver. I gasped, clenching as his fingers pressed into me, cold and thick.

"Relax, baby," he murmured. "You want this, right?"

And yeah, I did. I really fucking did, and I breathed through the pressure as Owen stretched me. His touch was firm but careful, and he was always asking what I needed. He had half his arm up my ass but he was respectful about it.

Fuck. This man. I was damn lucky to get lost in his cove...and then his bed.

I was in love with his fingers. It was just crazy, filthy love with those fingers. I could live out the rest of my days with nothing more than the sexual torment this man brought to me, and I would be content.

Correction: I *was* content. I needed nothing more.

"If you're gonna leak all over the place," Owen started, dragging his chin up my throbbing length, "I'm gonna have to lick you clean."

"You should," I replied. "It's your fault."

"And I'm happy to take responsibility," Owen said, laughing.

He swirled his tongue over the spot of arousal on my belly, and then took my cock in his mouth. He sucked and stroked in a slow, steady rhythm that had me moaning like a foghorn.

"Need to fuck you," he whispered against my thigh.

I nodded in response. I wanted that too, but there was

no reason to rush. My cock couldn't get any harder. It wasn't possible. And I was wrong; there *was* reason to rush and it had a lot to do with the orgasm winding its way down my spine. His teeth nipped at my inner thigh, and I was damn near floating when he bit down while his fingers circled my prostate.

"Oh my hell yes please," I cried.

Owen chuckled as he reached for the lube he'd left near my shoulder. He nudged my thighs open as his slippery fingers found my prostate again, and a hungry, desperate cry caught in my throat. "Get inside me," I growled. "Give it to me. Don't make me wait anymore."

I watched the rise and fall of Owen's chest as his cock replaced his fingers. When he pushed past my resistance, my gaze scraped up his body to his gorgeous face to see bliss softening his features. He leaned forward, his heat wrapping around me like a blanket as he braced his elbows on either side of my head. My hands went to his shoulders and my ankles to his ass as he thrust into me. His cheeks were flushed, his eyes hazed over with heat.

"Is this good?" he asked, flattening his hips against me. "Are you all right?"

I nodded, no words available to me. I was only capable of taking it, of taking him, and wanting him to take all of me in the process. Owen eased back, dragging his cock from me on a slow, torturous path. Our eyes met and then shifted downward, and we watched as he disappeared inside me again.

"Ah, *fuck*," he hissed.

He was fucking me slowly now, all rolling hips and

long, heavy thrusts, and I was about to lose my mind. I reached between us, suddenly frantic to find my release, and stroked my cock.

"No no," Owen said, moving my hands to his waist before taking my cock. "This is for me."

"But I need—"

"I know," he said, cutting me off with a kiss. "I know, little prince. But this is for me."

His grip was unforgiving, but his gaze. *Fuck*, that gaze. That was what got me. It was like he was staring straight into me, knowing me and begging me to know him in return. "Take it," I whispered. "Take all of me."

His thumb passed over my crown as he stroked into me. For a minute there, I went cross-eyed.

I'd never experienced sex like this before. There was the insanely good fucking component but that wasn't the whole story. It was the feeling of it all. The emotion behind every thrust, the intention in every kiss, the promise in every breath we shared. This kind of sex was an affirmation, and an ever-growing part of me knew I could scavenge the earth and not find anything else like it. Like *him*.

"Don't say something like that unless you mean it," Owen replied. "Because you better believe I will."

He did. He had me flying apart within minutes, one hot spurt after another.

"Your turn," I rasped, my eyes glued to his abs as they rippled with each glorious thrust. "You gave me everything I wanted, Owen. Now I want you to take what you need."

His eyebrows arched, and a smile tipped up one side of his mouth. He pulled out and jerked himself with the same force he'd offered me. It was a blur of movement and guttural moans, and he huffed out a long, filthy string of curses as his release hit. He spilled—and spilled and spilled—all over my belly.

"Look at you," he breathed as the last spasms spiraled through him. "Just look at you."

Owen swirled two fingers through the mess on my belly. I was warm all over, filled with a hot new happy that felt too good to be mine. "Come here," I whispered, pulling him to my side. "Just stay right there."

"Nowhere else I want to be," he murmured, his lips on my neck and shoulder.

I lived a pretty big life. I'd traveled the world and met celebrities, heads of state, and more billionaires than I could count. Even though there were moments when I wanted to kick it all to the curb, I had it good. But none of that life compared to Owen's head on my shoulder or his bare skin warming mine.

fifteen
OWEN

***Tacking:** v. To change course by turning a boat's head into and through the wind.*

WHERE OUR FIRST week of sleeping together was an overwhelming rush of new, urgent and rough in the best ways, we'd now eased into the lazy indulgence stage. There was no rush, no awkward moments. We had a feel for each other now, and we knew this wasn't ending at sunrise. That made all the difference.

Also, several nights of flat-out fucking combined with unrestricted touching throughout the day took some of the edge off. I could curl around Cole while our breathing eased and our bodies cooled, and not lose myself in another heady swirl of lust. It was a good thing I found that restraint, too. The afterglow left him chatty, but it wasn't his usual noise. He confessed his desires, shared secrets, told stories I was certain had never before seen the light of day.

It was another piece of Cole I was fortunate enough to claim as my own, and I relished these dark, quiet moments when we could shed everything and be the most raw versions of ourselves.

In all this glorious honesty and openness, a few critical details were missing. The reason for his extended summer vacation never came up. Details about his life in California were off the table. He rarely talked about his work, and when he did, it was to vent his hatred for corporate culture.

I knew I shouldn't but I preferred it this way.

I loved the fantasy of Cole. The version of him that came without strings or complications. That version didn't have a life and a business waiting for him on the other side of the country. That version wasn't going to gather up his pastel polo shirts and sail away.

If I could hold onto the fantasy, I wouldn't have to cope with the reality that I'd fallen for a man who could never be mine. Not really. I didn't need to know the inner workings of his world to know it wasn't mine. He could enjoy the hell out of a summer in Talbott's Cove, but that didn't mean he had any intention of permanently relocating here. Just another one of my sandcastle dreams. I was getting ahead of myself, planning our future together when I didn't know if he shared a fraction of my feelings.

I knew I was good for a fun time in the summer. That was how it went for me. I went starry-eyed and lovesick, and they went back to their lives in the city. Summer loves only led to autumn heartbreak, and that was why I needed the fantasy.

I blinked that thought away as I stared at the ceiling. It

was another hot, humid night and the ceiling fan only moved the oppressive air around. By all accounts, it was too hot for sex, for cuddling, for anything more energetic than lying flat on the bed and breathing. But none of that registered. It was as if my body didn't care to process anything but the feel of Cole's fingertips sliding over my hip. His head was on my chest, his arm around my waist, and his legs tangled between mine. The quilt was in a heap on the floor and the sheets were clinging to one corner of the mattress.

This, right here, was my heaven.

"Have you ever been with a woman?" he asked.

I shook my head. "No. Came close once," I admitted. "After that situation, it was pretty obvious I wasn't interested in the hetero scene." I brushed his damp hair off his forehead. "You?"

"Not...quite," he said.

"Go ahead and explain that one," I said, laughing.

Cole dragged his hand up my belly to the center of my chest and drummed his fingers there. "I was a little slutty in college."

"Slutty or experimental?" I asked.

He bobbed his head for a second, humming while he considered this. "Slutty," he replied with a laugh. "But also, experimental. Sluttily experimental, I guess."

"Was it fun?" I asked.

Cole hesitated. "Yeah, most of the time. Going away to college was a big change for me. I didn't know who I was back then, or how to be comfortable with myself. I was out then but I didn't know how my sexuality fit into my identity. I didn't know what it meant to embrace the feelings I'd had for so long, and then experience them with someone else. I didn't how to accept and embrace myself as a gay man. There were days when I struggled with it. I mean, I didn't walk around with a Pride pin on my jacket."

"You don't do that now," I said.

"And neither do you," he argued.

I stared at Cole, willing him to meet my eyes, but he didn't. "Fair enough," I replied. "Where does the experimentation come in?"

"College was like an all-you-can-eat sex buffet," he said. "Most of the time, it was with men, but there was one time with a woman. Sort of. Not completely."

I didn't want to hear this. I didn't, but I did. The thought of Cole with other men—a buffet of men, no less—twisted my gut. Cole with women was a different form of pain. I could hold my own when I was competing with gay guys for his affection, but I was powerless when it came to women. "All right. This woman. What's her story? Were you out with her?"

"I wasn't, no. I was still figuring out how to say it, believe it, own it back then. I made some mistakes along the way." He hesitated. "We were friends though it was clear she wanted to be more. She flirted with me all the time and always had a reason to touch me—"

"That's fantastic," I grumbled. This jealousy of mine, it knew no reason.

"She was all the right things—nice, funny, smart—but I wasn't into her," he said, ignoring me. "Not at all. Objectively, I knew she was beautiful and sexy—"

"Of course she was," I said under my breath.

He speared me with an amused smirk. "She was beautiful and sexy but I still wasn't into her," he continued. "She started seeing a guy. I figured she'd shift her attention toward him but it didn't work out that way. Instead, she wanted the three of us to hang out."

"Because they both wanted to fuck you," I said, not at all surprised by the bright streak of possession racing through my blood. "Right? Isn't that the way it worked out?"

Cole continued tapping his fingers against my breastbone, studying my skin without responding.

Eventually, he heaved out a sigh and said, "I didn't recognize that to the be the case at first, but yeah. That's what happened. Basically." He sanded his fingers through my chest hair. "It was just one time. I didn't do anything with her. Not really. The guy, though, he wanted to play. He was pretty enthusiastic about me introducing him to his prostate. She was cool with that but I'm certain she imagined herself as the star of the evening rather than the minor player. Looking back, I think she wanted to start a stable." He layered his hands over my heart, dropped his chin there, and met my eyes. "That was my first and last time with a woman. If you can even call that being *with* a woman. She went out of her way to avoid me after that. The guy hit me up every time he was lonely and drunk."

"I hate her," I said. "I'm not fond of him either."

Cole rolled away from me as he shook with laughter. "You shouldn't," he said between gasps. "It was several lifetimes ago. I hadn't thought about her in years."

"Yeah, well, I'm still not happy with her." I reached for him and caught hold of his backside. "Get back here," I ordered, pinching until he yelped.

"That's going to leave a mark," he said, glancing over his shoulder. "Remind me to never activate your jealous side."

"I'll kiss it better," I promised. "Sorry. I didn't expect you to tell me about a threesome with a side story about you fingering some virgin ass."

"Tell me about the time you came close with a woman, and I'll excuse it," Cole said, returning to his spot at my side. "Was it Annette?"

I clapped my hand over my eyes. "God. No," I said, groaning. "Not Annette." I shook my head and indulged in another groan. "I took one of Annette's best friends to the prom, Jenna, and then made a valiant effort at engaging in post-prom traditions. It was a disaster."

"I didn't even go to the prom," Cole said. "Never mind the after-party."

"You didn't miss anything," I promised. "I didn't want to go. My mom forced me. She picked out the tux, the corsage, the girl—"

"Wait a damn second," he interrupted, holding up his hand. "What did you just say? About your mother and the girl and the picking out?"

I pulled a pillow out from under my head and pressed it to my face. "My mom set me up," I replied, hoping the pillow would suffocate me quickly.

It didn't. He plucked it from my hands and tossed it across the room. "Why?" he asked.

"Let me ask you this," I said, sitting up against the headboard. "When you came out to your family, how'd that go? How did they react?"

"We're going to do that?" he asked. "We're going to trade coming-out stories now?"

"Answer the question, Cole."

He shifted to sit beside me, blinking at the sheets while he considered my question. "I didn't come out, not exactly," he admitted. "My dad and I were stuck in traffic one afternoon. He asked if I had any questions about safe sex, and whether I'd thought about my sexual orientation. That's why he said. *Sexual orientation*. At first, I was too stunned to say anything. No one had ever been that direct with me. Plenty of kids teased the shit out of me, and there was no shortage of bullies in school, but no one had ever stopped to ask me about my identity. They'd always made assumptions. Once I recovered from the shock, I told him I had thought about it, and I was attracted to men. He nodded, and lectured me on the limitations of condoms for twenty minutes."

A grim smile pulled at my lips while I bobbed my head. "And your mother? Your sisters? How did they take it?"

Cole shrugged. "My mom ordered a bunch of books about Stonewall, the AIDS crisis, and gay memoirs. She insisted we read and discuss them together. We watched *And the Band Played On*. That all sounds depressing, but it wasn't. I mean, not too depressing." He folded his hands in his lap. "My sisters baked me a Bundt cake."

"Yeah, that wasn't my experience," I said with a rueful laugh. "My dad was cool but my mom was convinced I was going through a phase. She said I was confused, and I didn't know what I wanted because I'd lived in this small town for too long. I didn't like the girls here because I'd grown up with them, and viewed them as sisters."

"That's terrible." He reached over and took my hand. "I'm sorry."

I shrugged off his words but laced our fingers together. "Honestly, I believe she meant well. She didn't see how I could know my sexual identity when I was a fifteen-year-old kid who'd never kissed a girl—or boy. She thought it was an exposure issue, and once I got some exposure, my outlook would change. That's why she was always setting me up on dates and telling girls I was just shy. She meant well," I repeated. "She just didn't understand."

"That doesn't make it any easier to swallow," Cole said. "Good intentions do not erase or excuse harmful actions."

"It's okay. I don't walk around with that rain cloud over my head," I said. "I might have Annette chasing after me, but I'm not deeply traumatized or anything."

"Hang on a second," Cole said, holding up a finger. "You've dated in this town, right?"

I barked out a laugh. "No," I said. "Never. This place is far too small for me to hook up with the locals. Hell, no."

"And that, my darling, is why Annette thinks you're free game," he said. "Think about it. Your mom told everyone you were confused, you don't date locally, and you're a gentleman of a certain age. Knowing all that, I'm not surprised the vagina vultures are circling."

"Gentleman of a certain age," I repeated. "Not sure how I feel about you calling me old, McClish."

"Shut up. It looks good on you," he said, dragging his gaze over my chest. "You need to shut it down with Annette. I see it from her perspective now, and you really need to shut it down."

I groaned. "Yeah, that sounds wonderful."

Cole shifted to face me. "Does she understand now? Your mom?"

I held my hands out as if I was weighing my thoughts. "Yes and no," I replied. "She was a guidance counselor at the local high school—"

"And she called it a phase. I'm dying a little inside right now," he murmured.

"After she retired from the high school, my parents moved to one of those master-planned communities for active adults not far from Miami," I replied. "She says she's learned a lot about 'the gays' living in south Florida. She recently asked if I had a drag name, and whether I liked twinks. Apparently, her hair stylist would be perfect for me."

"I'm dead," he murmured.

"She means well," I said, as much for Cole's reassurance as mine. "Even if she should've handled it differently when I came out, she didn't throw me on the streets. She didn't send me away to conversion camp. Talking about drag names isn't the best entry point but it's her way of reaching out. If there's one thing I've learned in my time on this planet, it's that I can't wait for people to be perfect. I can't reject them because they don't know the best way to open a discussion on my queer life. I can want more and demand more, but I'm not going to refuse them when they're trying."

"I wouldn't have expected that much tolerance from such a grumpy guy," he said.

I hooked my arm around his leg and yanked him closer. "What are you talking about? I'm not grumpy."

Cole snickered, bumping my ribs with his elbow. "No, of course not. You're salty. Surly. Moody. Curmudgeonly."

"Now you're just being mean," I said with a huff.

"Hardly," he quipped. "You don't like people."

I planted my hand on his chest and pushed him down to the mattress. Rising to my knees, I straddled his thigh. My cock was thick and heavy, and pulsing as I rutted on him. "I like you."

His abs dipped as a laugh moved through him. "Oh, what a relief," he replied. "One last question for you."

"It's never the last question," I grumbled.

He ran his knuckles up my arm with a soft laugh. "Maybe not," he conceded. "But *are* you into twinks? I want to know if I should be worried about this hair stylist. Or dieting."

I smiled down at him, all rippling muscles and golden skin, and shook my head. "No," I said, flattening my palm on his trim waist and dragging it up to his broad shoulders. "I'm not. I like my man thick," I said. "I'm gonna keep you that way."

sixteen

COLE

Snarl: *adj. The condition when two or more lobster lines become tangled.*

Neera: Could we schedule a check-in? Phone or video?
Cole: What would you like to discuss?
Neera: The usual. Goals, accomplishments, issues.
Cole: Nope.
Neera: Pardon me?
Cole: I'm not doing that. I don't have a work plan so I don't have goals, accomplishments, or issues to report back.
Neera: I thought you were developing something.
Cole: I am. But I'm not tying myself to timelines.
Neera: I see.
Cole: You say that when you don't see at all and just want to throw something at my head.

Neera: I wasn't attempting to imply that. I apologize.
Cole: No need to apologize.
Neera: Is there anything I can do to support you?
Cole: Not really. I'm being innovative. Isn't that my new job?
Neera: You're still dissatisfied. Still understandable.
Cole: If that's what you want to call it, that's fine.
Neera: What are you calling it?
Cole: I'm not. I'm just going about my life without agonizing over titles and hierarchy. There are more important things.
Neera: Such as?
Cole: Now that I think about it, there is something you can do.
Neera: I see you haven't lost your skill for deflection.
Cole: I'm going to send you a list of NGOs in need of some signal boosting. Some oceanic conservation nonprofits. Make it big but not connected to me.
Neera: I'll get right on it.

———

OWEN RAISED a hand toward the setting sun, waving at a passing lobster boat. The captain returned the gesture.

"That's the O'Keefe boat," he said, tipping his chin toward the green and white vessel. "They live north of town."

He ran his hand over my shoulder and I leaned into his touch. It was different now that we weren't working our asses off to avoid each other as a poor form of lust concealment. I enjoyed the easy affection he offered, and the freedom to reach for him whenever I wanted. It was a weightlessness I'd never before experienced, and it forced me to realize the ways in which I'd narrowed my life back in California.

I didn't date, I didn't flirt, I didn't have sex. There was no romance, no intimacy. I'd convinced myself I needed it that way. My existence was far too complex to add any human variables, and I was hardened by the fear of betrayal. Books featuring the sordid details of my company's inner workings—and my colorful leadership style—routinely landed on bestseller lists. Click-baity blogs went crazy every time I dined at a restaurant, splashing photos of me and my party. They'd make ridiculous comments about the people I was with and analyze the hell out of my meal. If they were lucky, they'd get a quote from a server about how much of an asshole I was that night.

There was no room in my world—the world I left in Silicon Valley—for a simple relationship. I couldn't determine whether I could change that world, make room. Whether Owen would be able to carry the weight of that world on his broad shoulders.

If I indulged in fanciful thoughts, I'd allow myself to believe I was meant to find Owen, and Talbott's Cove. I was meant to lose my title, leave California under the cover of PR bullshit, and nearly crash my boat on Maine's rocky coast.

If any of that was true and not merely the thing of fairy tales and dreams, I was also meant to tell Owen the truth about me and trust that his feelings wouldn't ebb. All this time in this cozy seaside town, all that had changed between us, and I still hadn't put my cards on the table with Owen. Not the ones that mattered, the ones revealing my true identity.

But it wasn't for lack of trying.

There was always something. An important ball game. A town council meeting. A breakthrough on one of my projects. A debate about nothing. A devious grin that turned into blowjobs behind the boat's bridge. Of course I could've put a stop to everything and forced him to listen but I didn't. With each passing day, it became more difficult to speak the truth when I'd let it linger in the shadows all this time.

When I was in college, one of my professors liked to say, "The longer you put off a task, the harder it is to get started." I couldn't remember the class but that adage stuck with me. I couldn't stop thinking about it, and watching the interest compound on this long overdue conversation.

"It's Thursday," I murmured. "Annette's staying open late for you."

Owen squeezed my shoulder, and I rubbed my cheek against his knuckles. "Don't remind me."

"Come on," I said, laughing. "You're a tough guy. You can handle a sweet little book mistress who hides her fangs incredibly well."

"Not sure about that," he said under his breath. "The fangs, that is. She's a nice lady. She means well."

"Another one with the good intentions." I ran my hand

down his back and slipped beneath the worn fabric of his t-shirt. "I'm sure there's a nice guy—one who likes vag—who will make her very happy."

Owen snickered. "Add that to your list of projects. Get on the dating websites and find Annette's perfect match. I'm sure you can make a spreadsheet or something. All scientific." He shifted to face me, a thoughtful wrinkle across his brow. "What are you working on? You never talk about your projects."

I cut my gaze toward the ocean as I answered, "Nothing you'd find interesting. Interfaces and apps, that kind of thing."

That was the truth. Mostly. It wasn't inaccurate. It only omitted a few details.

He nodded and turned his attention to the boat's controls as we headed in the direction of the fish market. I kept my hand on his back, right up against the strong dip where his torso disappeared under his shorts. I loved dragging my fingers through the dark patch of hair there.

"I am interested," he said quietly. "Just because I don't do the internet thing doesn't mean I don't care about your work."

"Oh," I managed, the sound sticking in my throat like a fish bone. "Oh, I know. I didn't mean to suggest—"

"You didn't," he interrupted, his words tempered with charity and patience. Two things Owen rarely offered. Two things I didn't deserve. "I know I've been something of an ogre about my low-tech lifestyle, and I'm sure it made you feel as though I didn't value your work." He stared at the docks in the distance as he chose his words.

"I didn't mean to make you feel unwelcome in any way. I'm sorry."

I couldn't believe this. If anyone was due to deliver an apology, it was me.

"You were not an ogre," I shot back.

"You can say it," he replied with a baleful shrug. "I was an ogre. It happens."

This was it. This had to be it. The last straw.

"Actually, we should talk about my business," I started. "There are a few things you should know."

Owen kept his gaze trained on the docks behind the fish market as he maneuvered around other lobster boats. "Yeah, if that's what you want," he said. "Let's finish up here and then you can give me the whole song and dance." He shot me a quick glance. "Will there be any singing or dancing? I get the impression you've got moves, McClish."

"What gives you that idea?" I replied, feigning a truckload of indignation.

Owen chuckled. "The way you move your hips when you like what you're getting. The way you shake your ass when you want my attention."

Was there anything that escaped Owen's notice? There couldn't be.

"Ass shaking aside," I started, sliding a hand down to give his rear end a squeeze, "we're going to the bookstore next."

I was stalling. Definitely stalling.

"The only reason you're pinching my ass is because you want me pounding yours," he warned.

I didn't respond until he stared at me for a moment.

"Are you waiting for me to deny it?" I asked. "If so, you're going to keep on waiting."

"Such a smart mouth on you. Where'd you say you went to school?"

"I didn't," I replied. "It's act one in the performance. You'll have to wait to find out, but not until after we visit your dear friend Annette."

"Then after that," he said, steering the boat into one of the empty slips. "It's not like you're going anywhere, right?"

"Right," I murmured.

"Toss those buoys over, would you?" Owen asked, pointing to the dock. "Go ahead and shake that ass a little while you do it."

———

"WHAT DOES ANNETTE HAVE FOR YOU?" I asked as we walked through Talbott's Cove's tiny downtown. "Other than a major crush and the names of the five children she wants to have with you."

"You're not funny," Owen murmured, shaking his head while he growled like an angry bear.

"You're cute when you're irritable," I replied. "Lucky for me, you're always irritable."

I glanced at the lovingly maintained sidewalk planters and window boxes on each storefront. This town, with its tavern, general store, inn, and short string of shops dotting the streets around the harbor, defined quaint. It was something out of a magazine, or one of those free calendars realtors liked to send their clients with idyllic scenes from far-off locations. Places that didn't seem real.

"Something about American Revolution battles," Owen said. He shoved his hands in his pockets and jerked his shoulders up as he spoke. "The untold stories and whatnot."

"You like history," I said, studying Owen for any reaction or gesture of agreement. I received none. "And literature."

"Do we really need an inquisition right now, McClish?"

Ah, my beast. There he was.

"I made two observations, Bartlett. That's hardly an inquisition. It would be an inquisition if I asked you to defend your preference for Whitman over Keats, or Melville over Joyce. An inquisition would be me asking you to explain why you'd want to explore the battles of the American Revolution when you probably covered them in high school, whereas you probably did not learn about the Belgian Revolution of 1789. A true inquisition would force you to attribute the success of the American Revolution to one influential individual—not George Washington—and compare that person to—"

"Enough," Owen roared as he ground to a halt. He tossed up his hands, ripped his baseball cap from his head, and ran his hands through his hair. "I'm not in the mood to choke on your huge IQ right now."

I continued for several steps before stopping and pivoting to stare at him. His hands were perched on his hips and I could almost see the waves of frustration radiating from his body. If I didn't know him better, I'd think he was about to go Hulk Smash on this town. But I was beginning to believe that I did know him, and I knew he liked it when I pushed him. When I forced him to interact with me despite his desire to retreat into his thoughts. When he needed to get out of his head—and his worries about damaging Annette's feelings—for a minute.

"But my huge dick?" I asked, waving toward him. "You'd choke on that?"

"Like it's my job." Owen advanced on me, swallowing up the sidewalk in two long strides, and snatched my hand. "Let's get this over with. You'll get your inquisition later."

I followed him into the small shop, a bell tinkling overhead as we entered. I zeroed in on Annette as I crossed the threshold. She was behind the counter, her dark hair spilling over her shoulders, making her white dress appear strapless. It was the sexy angel look, and she was nailing it.

A customer stood on the other side of the counter, nodding while she spoke and held up each item in his pile, turned it over, opened the jacket, then patted the front cover. It appeared that she was telling him the secrets behind every book, offering up the special details only a bookseller would know.

If I wasn't busy stewing in jealousy over her baseless stake on my man, I'd want to get to know her. The lady was high octane, and I liked that. I respected it. I also had the distinct impression she had dirt on everyone in this small town, and I respected that, too.

"We'll just wait," Owen said, glancing at Annette before turning away. "I'm sure it will be only a minute."

"She talks with her hands," I said under my breath. "Five bucks says it will not be a minute."

"Shut up," he whispered.

The space was flooded with sunlight and books, paperbacks and hardcovers overflowing from every surface. A quick scan of the covers told me I wasn't the subject of any of these books, and that was a relief. Cheerfully painted terra cotta pots and baskets marked the new release section. Hand-drawn signs announced sections for every subgenre. Maine was well represented. There was local history, local cookbooks, local fiction, local nonfiction, local photography, even local romance.

"See anything you like?" Owen asked, squeezing my hand. "Oh—right. You don't read real books."

"That kind of incendiary language is unnecessary," I replied, smirking. "Since you know all the best reads around here, pick something out for me. You know what I like."

His answering smile was dark, almost feral. "Yeah, I do." He inclined his head toward the opposite side of the shop, tugging my hand. "Let's see what we can find for you, little prince."

We crossed the small sales floor toward a section cheerfully labeled with a hand-lettered pennant banner as mystery and suspense. Owen stood behind me, one hand on my waist while he skimmed his free hand over the book spines. His breath was warm on my neck and the scruffy tickle of his beard sent a shiver through my shoulders.

"This is going to be good," I said. "We'll have a little

book club situation going. Can we have wine and cheese with our literary conversations?"

He tugged a paperback from the shelf, ignoring me. "This might work," he said, almost to himself. "Cybercrimes. International intrigue. A bit of a love story."

"That's what I like?" I asked, arching back to press my ass to his crotch. "Tech stuff and spy games? Sounds like my day job."

"You forgot the part about the love story," he replied, his words rougher than they were a moment ago.

I laughed. "None of that in my day job."

Owen's arm curled around my torso, his fingers sliding barely beneath my shorts. He pressed his lips to my neck. "Good," he said. "You should save that part for your summer vacation."

I almost replied, telling him that I *had* saved the love story for this summer vacation, and that he was playing a starring role.

But Annette called, "It's my favorite fishermen!" and the words dried on my tongue.

With a sigh, I dropped my head back to Owen's chest. He pulled his fingers from beneath the waistband of my shorts but I clamped my hand over his, stopping him. "Where do you think you're going?"

"I'm not going to molest you in public," he snapped.

Annette rounded the counter, her perky smile melting into a confused grimace as she approached.

"You've done it before." I hooked my hand around the back of his neck, pulling his face closer. "Kiss me," I ordered. "Right now."

Owen didn't hesitate. His lips met mine with a kiss that started sweet and turned molten in seconds. But neither of us forgot we were in this shop, not more than a few feet from the woman who'd been crushing on my man for ages. With one last peck and a hungry growl, he broke away.

"Hey, Annette," Owen said.

His pinky finger was still in my shorts, and in some small, strange way, that was a victory for us.

Annette hugged a hardcover book to her chest and she blinked at us. Repeatedly. Her gaze followed Owen's hold on my body, each blink growing longer and more exaggerated. It was as though she was trying to erase the image in front of her by closing her eyes and wishing it away.

A fraction of me felt badly for her. I didn't need to have a long balance sheet of heartbreak behind me to know she was watching a relationship end. Even if that relationship was one-sided and nonexistent.

"Good to see you, Owen," she said, a dejected sigh weaving through her words. "You too, Cole."

"You have a great shop," I said. "Awesome selection, fantastic layout."

"Yeah, I try," she said. She glanced away and touched her fingertips to her brow, brushing aside a lock of hair. "Is there anything I can help you find?"

"I think we're good," I replied at the same moment Owen said, "Cole wants a few mystery novels. Can you recommend some?"

"Oh," Annette said, surprised. "Oh, sure." She took one hesitant step forward, another, and then she was scurrying around the store.

"Look what you did now," I whispered to Owen. "You activated her hummingbird setting."

"Me?" he asked, his head swiveling as he watched Annette. "This is definitely your fault."

"Only because I wouldn't let you lead this woman on for another decade," I replied. "We could've paid for your book and left, but you laid down the bookish lady challenge instead and now she's trying to prove a point."

She flew around us, snatching up books and tucking them under her arm as she stomped. "Let me pick out some books for your new boyfriend, Owen. That's what I do, make everyone else happy. Sure! Mysteries. Fantastic! Everyone else gets their happy and I get to pick out books. Fabulous!"

"So," I murmured. "This is really happening."

"It is, and I don't like being the asshole in her story," Owen said to me.

"Mysteries. I love a mystery. Sometimes I think I live in a mystery. You know, the *what is happening in my life?* mystery. Because I sure as hell don't know." She slammed a pile of books on the counter. "Can I get you anything else?"

"No, this is plenty," I replied while Owen said, "Did that special order come in?"

From her position behind the counter, Annette seemed to deflate. Her shoulders fell, her jaw unclenched, her grimace wilted into a frown. "Yeah, Owen, it did," she said. "I'll need a minute, okay?"

She didn't wait for a response, instead smoothing her hands down her skirt, turning around, and heading for the back room.

"It would've been easier to let her think we had a chance," Owen said, loosening his hold on me. "That would've been better than this."

Owen shook his head and walked toward the butcher block counter where the cash register was located, leaving me to chase after him.

"No, it would *not* have been better," I replied. "You can't continue that way. It's not right, and it's not fair to you."

"It's fine and—"

"It's not fair to me," I interrupted. "It would be one thing if she had a simple crush on you. But it's not a simple crush. It's not the same as that girl at the fish market in Bar Harbor who eye-fucks you every time we stop in. Hell, I've seen half the women on the seacoast undress you with their eyes. That's a different story. It's temporary. This is hitching her hopes to your dick and waiting for you to learn to like the feel of it."

Owen stared at me, his expression impassive as always. Then, "Okay. You're right," he said. "But you should know the other half of the women on the seacoast undress *you* with their eyes."

Annette emerged from the back room, a book in hand and smudged mascara under her eyes. "Here we go," she said, adding the paperback to our towering pile.

"Annette," Owen started, "about all of this. I didn't mean to make you uncomfortable. If I did, I'm...I'm sorry."

She waved away his words with both hands, shaking her head. "No apologies needed. I wasn't thinking. I wasn't being smart," she said. Then, softly, "I knew but I still hoped."

They stared at each other, Owen with his furrowed *I don't want to hurt you* brows and Annette with her big, tear-filled Disney princess eyes. A different iteration of me would've offered a pithy remark, something intended to cut the tension and trivialize the moment. I couldn't do that. I cared about Owen, enough to march him into this face-off. Instead, I scanned the immediate area and found a display of Maine coastline photography books. I grabbed three copies.

"This looks like something my mother would love. My sisters, too," I announced.

Annette dragged her gaze away from Owen only to shoot me the most unimpressed glare in the modern history.

"My mother loves a good coffee table book," I continued. This much was true. "She likes to dig through the clearance piles at her local bookstore. For reasons I don't understand, she hates paying sticker price for anything. Unfortunately, she doesn't live in a region where bartering is part of the cultural norms. She lives in Palm Springs. It's hotter than hell there. Come to think of it, I have a funny story about that."

It was Owen's turn to scowl at me. The upside? They weren't locked in some Romeo-and-Juliet-but-one-of-them-is-gay trance anymore.

"My mother plays tennis with a former Catholic priest," I said, waving my arm as though I was holding a racquet. "They play tennis and then drink boxed wine spritzers. White zin and store-brand seltzer. I don't know how they found each other or why he left the priesthood, but it's sufficient to say they're good friends now."

"Please tell me there's a point to this," Owen said.

Ignoring him, I continued, "The priest—rather, former priest—has an old story about missionaries traveling west. The Church would send one party of missionaries after another to the desert, but they couldn't convert anyone. When asked why it was so difficult, one of the missionaries explained the people in that region didn't need religion because half the year gave them everything they needed to know about heaven and the other half gave them everything they needed to know about hell."

"Great," Annette said, still unimpressed.

Chuckling, Owen roped his arm around my waist. "You talk too damn much."

"I'll just ring these up and you two can be on your way." She glanced up, working hard at a sunny smile that just wasn't there. "Will these be together or separate?"

Owen caught my eye, smiling despite Annette's increasing distress. "Together." He bowed his head toward my ear, whispering, "When we get home, I'm gonna torture you for several hours."

I was all too happy to oblige. "You should do that," I said, keeping my voice low. "Torture. Punish. Subjugate. Whatever you want."

Owen's gaze shifted to Annette and then back to me. "Don't say that," he murmured. "You don't know what I'm thinking."

"That will be one-forty-four fifty," Annette said, glancing between us.

I grinned. "I have an idea," I replied to Owen, pulling my wallet from my back pocket. I handed her my credit card without tearing my eyes away from him. "I have several ideas, actually. I'm in favor of all of them."

seventeen

OWEN

***Keel:** n. The longitudinal structure along the centerline at the bottom of a vessel's hull, on which the rest of the hull is built, in some vessels extended downward as a blade or ridge to increase stability.*

THE MOON WAS high in the sky, a cool breeze was blowing in off the water, and a choir of cicadas screeched in the distance. My body was spectacularly sated and my man was wrapped around me, still purring from the pounding I'd given him.

This life, it didn't get much better.

Drunk on that milky afterglow, I stared at Cole's blond hair and sun-kissed skin and willed myself to withhold the declarations of love and forever I itched to give him. It was too soon for any of that, and if he didn't enthusiastically reciprocate, I doubted I'd recover from the blow.

Instead, I dug into my plentiful stores of jealousy, asking, "What changed for you?"

"What? When?" he asked. His words were rough, his voice raw from hours of begging and moaning.

Lord, I liked that. I liked the marks I'd sucked into his neck, chest, thighs. I liked the beard rash between his legs. I liked the red, swollen shape of his lips. He'd be sore tomorrow, his body used in delicious ways, and I'd like that, too.

For as much as I enjoyed the evidence, I enjoyed caring for him more. Soaping him up in a steamy shower. Rubbing him down with thick creams and herby balms. Kneading his tender muscles. Kissing it all better.

I patted his backside. "You said you were slutty in college, but then you wind up in the Cove and you're a born-again virgin. What changed?" I asked.

"Mmhmm." He nodded, his scruffy chin scraping my chest. "I founded a technology firm, one that gained a certain amount of ubiquity. Most people think it's all about hatching a new idea and then watching the cash roll in, but that isn't a tenth of the truth. That new idea has to stay new, stay fresh. It has to evolve faster than its users, and it has to anticipate needs. Shareholders expect innovation but they also demand robust earnings. There are always disasters. Every day, a new crisis."

I nodded, but I didn't know what to say.

"And I've...I've made some mistakes," Cole said. "Years ago, when I was just starting out, I trusted someone. I shouldn't have done that."

I shifted to catch his gaze. "Who do I have to kill?"

Cole offered a weak laugh. "It's in the past. It doesn't matter now."

"The past has a way of staying present," I said.

"Especially when there's litigation involved," Cole said. "We were close. Friends, then lovers, and then he was an essential member of my team. He took confidential information about my business—about me—and sold it to the highest bidder." He blew out a heavy sigh. "I've had a few hookups since then but nothing more than that."

A surprised breath burst from my lips. I didn't know what I expected Cole to tell me, but it wasn't that. "Are you kidding me? Someone did that to you?"

"That doesn't even scratch the surface, babe." He shook his head against my chest. "This can't make much sense without the full context," he said. "Silicon Valley is a complex place, and my firm—

"Cole, stop," I interrupted. I wanted to know just enough, but not everything. "I understand what you're saying. You don't have to explain all the bits and pieces to me."

He tipped his face up, his brow wrinkled as if he'd misheard me. "I don't?"

I stared out the window for a long moment. When I was a kid, I believed all manner of sea monsters lived in the Atlantic's deep, cold waters. They were out there, swallowing up boats and fighting whales and sharks. In my kid brain, I convinced myself that I was safe as long as I could see the shoreline. Monsters never dared to enter the tidal zone.

That was how I felt about Cole, and the life he led separate from me. If we stayed on familiar ground, we'd be safe.

"You own a technology firm," I said.

"Fifty-one percent of it," he added. "My founding team and the shareholders own the rest."

"You own most of a technology firm," I started, "and a dickhead guy screwed you over. That's all I need to know."

Even after all these years working the water, part of me still believed in the great, unknown sea monsters. Beasts that would sneak up and strike without warning.

"Are you sure about that?" Cole asked.

"I am. I want Cole, the lost sailor. The man overboard. The guy who intrudes on my jerkoff sessions," I said with a chuckle. "Let's not muck this up with too much reality. Okay?"

Cole tipped his face up and stared at me, his lips folded in a tight line and his brows still wrinkled. For a second, I thought he was going to call me on my bullshit. Hold up my objections as illogical and unreasonable, and something I'd never accept if he tried to pull the same maneuver. But he pressed his palm to my heart, gave me a quick smile, and said, "Okay."

"Okay?" I repeated.

"Yeah, talking about corporate shit stresses me out," he replied. "I'd rather hear about you. Why hasn't some guy snapped you up? You're one helluva cook, you bathe regularly, and you have the baddest sex toy box. That's the full bear package right there."

I dropped my head back on the pillow and stared at the

ceiling while a soft laugh rolled through my chest. "Maybe I don't want to be snapped."

"Everyone wants to be snapped," Cole replied. "There's no one in the world who doesn't want it. We want it in different ways, at different times, but we still want it. *Need* it, even when we say we don't. We want to be accepted, cherished, adored. We want someone to recognize our messy, complicated souls, and love us for those messes and complications."

"Maybe," I conceded. "But some people just want to get fucked while they're on vacation."

"Are you talking about me?" Cole pushed off my chest and glared down at me. "You know I didn't even bring lube with me. I didn't come here expecting to get fucked."

I hooked my arms around his torso and returned him to my chest. "No, I'm not talking about you, silly boy," I said. "But you're not the first guy to spend the summer in Maine. Too many times, I've fallen hard for some pretty young thing, only for him to leave at the end of the summer without a backward glance. It's vacationland for them, and vacations never last."

Cole planted small kisses along my sternum, humming as he went. "I'm sorry, babe."

"They always went back to their girlfriends, too," I grumbled.

"I hate them," he hissed. "They didn't deserve you, or your gold-medal dick."

I wrapped my arms around him as a laugh rocked through me. "Gold-medal dick? *That* good?"

Cole snorted. "You know I'm not going to be able to sit

for a week," he said. "Aside from those pretty young things, hasn't anyone else tried to keep you?"

"I don't want to be kept," I said, immediately hating the tense of my words. *Didn't* want. *Didn't*. But I couldn't take it back now, and I couldn't color my relationship history to suit my purposes. "There's a vibrant queer community in Portland. The West End side of downtown has some great bars and restaurants, and I meet up with friends about once a month. Sometimes, I hookup with a fuck buddy. It's not a big deal."

Cole was silent for a moment, then he asked, "Am I your fuck buddy? Is that what we're doing?"

I sanded my fingers through his hair, hoping my touch could speak all the words I wasn't ready to say and he wasn't ready to hear. "No. You're my little prince."

He nodded. "I can live with that."

eighteen
COLE

Sextant: *n. A navigational instrument used to measure a vessel's latitude.*

Cole: Another request.
Neera: What do you have for me?
Cole: Can you push an independent bookstore package for the homepage?
Neera: Of course. Any other parameters?
Cole: Good bookstores. Not pretentious, snotty joints but community-based, inclusive, representative. All that good stuff.
Cole: Make sure Harborside Books in Talbott's Cove, Maine gets top billing.
Neera: Should we mention you're a fan of that shop?
Cole: Nope.
Neera: Understood.
Cole: If there's an opportunity to run some content on

women entrepreneurs or female-owned businesses, get that one on the list.
Neera: Consider it done.
Cole: Thank you.
Cole: And thank you for keeping the questions at a minimum.

———

Neera: I apologize if this is too forward but...are you all right?
Cole: Great. Why?
Neera: It takes you days to reply to messages, and that's highly atypical.
Neera: You're also calmer than I expected.
Cole: Were you expecting me to give a ranty interview to Fast Company or show up at the campus with Dumbledore's Army to oust my replacement?
Neera: Somewhat, yes.
Neera: Are you planning something like that?
Cole: No.
Neera: That's it? No?
Cole: Yeah. No. I have other things on my mind right now.
Neera: Does that include some new programming?
Cole: I'm staying out of trouble. You do the same.
Cole: No. Forget that. You could use some trouble in your life.
Neera: Pardon me?
Cole: Do something fun. Get away from the Valley. There is a whole wide wonderful world outside the Valley.

Neera: So I've heard.

Cole: Get out of the office. It will do you good.

Neera: Says the man who had to be forced onto a luxury sailboat.

Cole: I never appreciated how good it is to get away until I was required to do it.

Cole: Before you say anything, no, leadership retreats in Banff or Sun Valley don't count. Neither does the Appalachian incident. Those were all work. This place is different. It's good for me.

Neera: Thank you for that clarification.

Cole: It occurs to me that you might enjoy some forced time off. Should I fire you? Would that help?

Neera: We've talked about this. It's not acceptable to threaten termination in casual conversation.

Cole: That's right. My bad.

nineteen

COLE

Heeling: v. To be tilted temporarily by the pressure of wind or by an uneven distribution of weight on board.

THE LONG SUMMER days were giving way to later sunrises and earlier sunsets, and the woods behind Owen's house were turning fiery and golden. Autumn was right around the corner, and it dawned on me that I hadn't paused to admire the passing of a season since childhood. These days, I couldn't miss it. Everything about my life —*our* life—in this quiet town was tuned in to the nature's every turn.

I used to think I knew what I wanted, and I knew where I wanted to be. The brightest, most forward-thinking mind in Silicon Valley. The dominant force in my industry. People hanging on my every word. Big house, fast cars, influential friends. More money than I'd be able to spend in a hundred lifetimes.

Somewhere along the way, the operative features of my life lost their relevance.

Being demoted had something to do with it, but losing my way in the North Atlantic and sailing to Owen and the Cove claimed a large share of the responsibility. After six weeks here, I knew it to be true. If I hadn't found myself here, I would've spent a few weeks on the water, raging my way from one seasonal town to another while I cooked up a plan to retake my company.

I would've done it. Abandon the boat, fly back to California, storm into the office, and argue the shit right out of my replacement. I would've screamed, thrown things, caused a dreadful scene. And for several precious moments, I would've felt better, too. Vindicated, even.

But that tantrum wouldn't have made a damn bit of difference. It would've only confirmed for my board of directors that they'd made the right call.

Now, from the comfort of Owen's guest room, I was thankful for the upheaval I'd experienced this summer. I was no longer resentful of the board's decision to remove me as CEO. With my fingers flying over my keyboard as I blew through line after line of the best code I'd constructed in years, I appreciated their decision. They saw everything I wasn't willing to accept—my inability to care about every little financial indicator, my fraught relationship with strategic decision making, my curious management style —and enacted changes I never would've made on my own.

Most of the time, I was the smartest guy around. I was

used to that. It'd always been that way. There was nothing I couldn't accomplish if I worked hard enough, stretched my skills, learned something new. Knowledge was my belief system, and the one that convinced me I could do anything and everything.

The only trouble with knowledge was that it never stopped to ask if I wanted to do everything.

I didn't, and recognizing that truth was like taking my first deep breath in decades. My head cleared, my senses sharpened, and my heart pounded with the promise of my man's unyielding affection. This was where I belonged, and I wanted to celebrate that. Get out of the house, go places, see people, let them see me. See *us*.

For all the time we spent joined at the hip, I wasn't convinced the people of Talbott's Cove saw us as a couple. I meant to change that tonight.

I saved my work and yanked the noise-canceling headphones off. I pushed my glasses to the top of my head and stretched my arms out in front of me.

Once I stowed my gear, I left the bedroom and went in search of Owen. I found him in the kitchen, his hands braced on the countertop while he stood, reading the local newspaper. Instead of standing beside him, I roped my arms around his waist, pressed my chest to his back, and nuzzled his neck. "Let's go out," I murmured.

"You're rubbing your dick on my ass and you want to go out?" he asked. "Seems contradictory, McClish."

"I want to go out with you," I insisted, my lips sliding under his ear.

Owen barked out a laugh, the sound reverberating

through his body and into mine. "You want to take me on a date?" he asked over his shoulder.

I stole the opportunity to drop a kiss on his lips. "We enjoyed ourselves the last time we went out. Let's do that again."

"Are we going on a date?" he asked, reaching back to grip my neck. "Or do you want to get naughty in the woods?"

"Yeah, I want to take you out on a date," I replied with a purposeful roll of my hips against his backside. "And I want to show off my man."

He chuckled, a rough, rich sound that went straight to my cock. "Show me off? Why?"

"I want everyone to know you're off the market."

"What would that involve?" he asked. "I don't think JJ at The Galley would put up with you blowing me on the bar."

I rested my forehead between his shoulder blades, laughing. "I wouldn't blow you on the bar," I replied against his shirt. "I'd do it in a booth. Like a gentleman."

"Good to know," Owen replied, a laugh ringing in his words. "So, we're doing this? We're going on an actual date?"

"A real date with date-ish things," I said. "I'll pull out your chair for you, we'll engage in pleasant conversation, and maybe I'll let you kiss me goodnight at the door."

"By 'kiss you at the door,' do you mean fuck you in the woods?"

I slipped my hand between his legs, stroking him over his shorts. "I see no problem with that interpretation."

He reached back and squeezed my ass. "Go pick out a shirt for me. I want to be presentable for my date."

I nodded against his back but didn't let him go. "Are you sure about this?" I asked. "You don't mind being *with me* in the village?"

Owen was quiet for a long moment, his fingers still gripping my backside. Eventually, he said, "No. I don't hide who I am, and I don't want to hide you."

twenty
OWEN

Swinging the Lamp: *v. Telling sea stories.*

WE WALKED TO THE VILLAGE, following the worn path through the woods. Fingers of sunlight cut through the canopy, turning the woods into a bright, breezy stroll absent of the dark seduction we'd shared all those weeks ago.

"How's the project going?" I asked, shooting a glance at Cole as we neared the end of the trail. "It seemed like you were really focused today."

He bobbed his head. "It's good. Really good. I'm making a lot of progress."

I hesitated. I hated to tempt fate by inquiring about his work. "What happens when you finish?" I asked. "Does that mean—will you go back to California when you're done?"

"That's the beauty of the internet, Bartlett," Cole said, a bright smile stretched across his gorgeous face. "I can do this from anywhere in the world."

It was an answer but it wasn't. It didn't escape my notice that I was exceedingly sensitive about this topic, too. Any waffling from Cole, and I was bracing for impact.

"As long as you don't mind," he added. "I don't want to overstay my welcome."

"I am getting free labor out of you," I said. "It's not good labor but it is free. I can't complain."

"Such a grumpy motherfucker," he murmured.

I held The Galley's door open and gestured for Cole to enter. "Isn't this the way we're supposed to do it?" I asked. "Since we're on a date."

"If this is a date," Cole started, "you should check out my ass while I walk by."

He walked through the doorway, glancing over his shoulder to verify I was ogling him. "I don't need an occasion to check out your ass," I said, sliding my hand into his back pocket. "But since you asked, you're looking fine as fuck in those shorts."

I'd never stopped myself from touching him, not since I'd gained the right. I'd never given much thought to who might notice, but tonight was different. I wanted everyone to notice.

He smiled over at me, preening a bit, but my gaze was on the woman tucked into the far corner of the bar with an open book at her elbow. It had been weeks since that exceedingly awkward exchange with Annette in the bookstore. We'd seen her around town, of course, but our paths hadn't crossed. Until now.

Cole followed my stare, humming in acknowledgement. "She seems busy," he said. "We should leave her alone. If she wants to chat, she'll stop by."

Nodding, I walked with him to an open booth. We sat facing each other, his hand over mine, and debated beers.

"I want to try the shandy," he said, his brows furrowed in thought as he studied the menu.

"Please don't," I replied. "It's not right to mix beer with lemonade. It's a crime against reason."

"But I don't like hoppy beers," he argued. "The ones you drink, they're like liquid pinecone."

Absently, he ran his thumb over his bottom lip. I wanted to jump across the table and do the same, if for no other reason than I hadn't felt that lip in the past half hour.

"Then try a Belgian wheat. If you're nice, JJ will throw a slice of orange in there for you," I said. "It will taste the same if you close your eyes."

Cole glanced at me, his lips quirking up into a smirk. "Are we still talking about beer?"

I barked out a laugh. "Mostly," I replied. "The same could be said for balls."

"That is false." He pointed at the menu, a silent command to focus on my ale of choice rather than his mouth.

"All right," I said after the waitress took our drink orders. A Juliet Imperial Stout for me, a Night Swim'ah for him. "Let's date night the shit out of this."

"Do you come here often?" Cole asked, fighting a grin. He couldn't manage a straight face. He winked and God help me, it unleashed a rush of butterflies in my belly. I was in it deep with this man. "Forget that. Tell me about yourself, Bartlett. Tell me things you've never told me before. All the things we skipped. The basics. What d'you do for fun?"

I held out my hands and then let them fall. "Reading. I like books, but you already know that."

"But I don't know why you like it," he said. "Start there."

"I blew off school when I was a kid but now I wish I'd paid more attention," I said. "If I knew then what I know now, I wouldn't have pissed away my time."

"We're never given things when we want them," Cole said. "It's the universe's way of fucking with us."

"Something like that," I said, laughing.

Cole reached for his beer, asking, "When was the last time you took a vacation? I can't imagine lobstermen observe traditional holidays. The lobsters don't give a fuck whether it's Christmas or Columbus Day, right?"

"It can be challenging, yeah. But I got away a couple of months ago," I replied. "I sail down to Provincetown—that's in Massachusetts, on the far end of Cape Cod—every year for Pride. The past few years, I've rented a house with a bunch of guys. It's always a good time in P-Town. Parades, events, shows. It's a trip I never miss."

"Why? What makes it important?" Cole asked.

"It's like coming home, but instead of parents and

siblings, it's people who welcome and accept you in the most thorough way. And you've slept with most of them at one point or another." I ran my knuckles over my jaw as I watched him take in this information. The hard set of his jaw and thin line of his lips told me he wasn't a fan of my past exploits. "Have you ever been to Pride?"

He blew out a breath, his expression turning pensive. "No, I haven't." He reached for his glass but didn't drink. "I've never known how I'd fit in. If I'd fit in."

"Trust me, you and your slim-fit polo shirts will fit right in," I replied, laughing. "Maybe...you could come with me next June. We could go together."

"Yeah. Maybe," he said, bobbing his head slowly. "These friends of yours—the ones you've slept with—would we stay with them? Is that what we'd do? A bunch of us in a house? Musical beds, perhaps?"

I crossed my arms over my chest. "Is that your way of asking whether I'd share you?"

Cole lifted a shoulder while he drew lines in the condensation on his glass. "I'm just trying to understand how it goes," he replied.

"No, it wouldn't be like that," I said, dead serious. "If we bunked with my buddies, I'd bite your neck and piss a circle around you to make my intentions clear. Hell, I'd do that regardless of where we stayed. Your fine ass wouldn't leave my sight."

His cheeks flushed red, and I liked that. He bit his lip to hold back a smile, but it didn't work. I took his hand in mine just to feel an ounce of that electricity.

"All right. Good to know," he said. "Aside from that celebration, do you get away from the Cove much?"

"I take long weekends when I can," I said. "It seems like I'm always going to weddings. Back before marriage equality was passed nationwide, it was legal in Massachusetts. Many of my friends went there to get married, so I was always sailing down to the Cape." I glanced down, suddenly feeling shy. "I did the internet minister thing a couple of years ago. I've officiated for some of my friends. A few people in town, too."

Cole blinked at me, silent for longer than comfortable in this type of conversation. "That's—that's amazing," he replied.

"You really think so?"

"Yes," he said, slapping both hands on the table. "I want to hear all about this. How did you start?"

I rubbed my neck, thinking back. "It all started when some friends from Portland were planning their wedding and they couldn't find an officiant they liked. They wanted someone who knew them and actually gave a shit about them taking this step in their relationship. For reasons I still don't understand, they decided I was the guy for the job."

"And you kept going?" Cole asked. "After that wedding, you kept officiating?"

"Pretty much," I said. "I didn't set out with the intention of starting a side hustle in the wedding business, but I'm happy to take part in these special days."

He shifted, leaning out of the booth and peering

around the tavern. "I want to know who you've married here," he said. "You've got me hooked on townie gossip."

I held out my hand, ticking off each couple on my fingers. "The harbormaster and his wife. It was the second marriage for both of them. If you believe the rumors, they filed for divorce because they were cheating on their partners with each other. Now," I said, pausing, "I can't tell you whether those rumors are true but I know they got together right after their divorces, and they were engaged a month later."

"Huh," Cole murmured. "He's a nice guy. I haven't met the wife."

"She's a physician's assistant a few towns south of here." I held up another finger. "The couple that runs the inn. They bought the old motel about eight, maybe nine years ago, and fixed it up. They don't have any family. They moved up here for a fresh start after a gruesome tragedy. I don't know the particulars, only that it was bad. It seemed only right to offer my services to them."

"Whoa," he murmured. "I can't believe you've never mentioned this. The innkeepers with the horrible history *and* you moonlighting as a minister. All this time, and you've kept this incredible side of yourself hidden."

I took a sip of my beer as I considered Cole's comment. "I'm not like most people," I said carefully. "I don't feel the need to post all my thoughts and experiences on the internet, or see anyone else's thoughts and experiences. I'd rather take my time to understand someone piece by piece. I don't want to condense anyone down to a blurb or caption. I want to hold and treasure every piece, and I want someone to do the same to me."

Cole brought his fingers to his eyelids. He laughed, but I couldn't imagine why. Unless he thought I was an antiquated fool. That was entirely possible.

"I am so happy we're doing this," he said, dragging his hands down his face. "I'm truly amazed by you, and I want to hear more."

My eyebrows arched up. "Really?"

"Let me hold and treasure this piece of you," he said. Warm sensation rippled down my spine with his words. "Okay?"

"There was a couple I met a few years ago," I said, resting my head back on the booth. "Two of the strangest people I've ever met but I've never forgotten them."

"What made them so strange?" he asked, his face split in a warm smile.

I shook my head, still struggling to put those two into words even after several years. "To start, they were wandering around the docks in Wellfleet at four in the morning. He's a doctor, she's some kind of scientist, and they wanted me to take them on as deckhands for the haul. At first, I thought they were high on Ecstasy or something. Turned out, they were just really fucking weird."

"You are always short-staffed, aren't you?"

I waved him off. "I don't work the water when I'm outside of the Cove, but there's an old timer down there who had a hip replacement that year. A bunch of us pitched in to help him out so he could cover his costs. It was just one weekend. I didn't need a full crew for that."

"Okay, now that we've established you're the nicest guy in the world," Cole said, gesturing to me, "tell me about this strange couple."

"From the first moment, they were like magnets. Chemistry so intense I could see it radiating off them. What they had, it was palpable. Part of me was jealous," I admitted. "But the other part of me was happy I was able to stand in the presence of real, limitless love. Even if they were annoying."

"You married them? On the boat, at four in the morning?" Cole asked. "How did that work, legally? If they were wandering around the docks, they couldn't have had a proper marriage license."

"I married them while the sun rose over Cape Cod Bay. It was one of the coolest ceremonies," I said. "It wasn't legal, but that wasn't an issue for them. They belonged to each other and it didn't matter whether they had the documentation to back it up."

Cole laughed. "Now I'm jealous of them, too."

"The strangest part came last year," I continued. "It was December, a couple days before Christmas, and they showed up at my door. I still don't know how they found me."

"That *is* strange," he said.

"They wanted to make it legal," I said. "I married them again. This time, I did it in the middle of my kitchen."

"Knowing how you react when people show up at your house uninvited," Cole mused, "you must really like weddings."

"Only certain weddings," I replied. "I only marry

people I can see staying together for the long haul. I've passed on officiating for folks who didn't seem right for each other, or ready for the commitment. The ones who just want a party. The ones who need something to do. The ones who think it's the next milestone they should check off in their life. I don't want to be associated with any marriages that end, you know?"

"Does that mean you believe everyone has a lobster?"

"A *what*?" I asked.

"You know, a lobster," Cole said, laughing. "From that episode of *Friends*. Lobsters mate for life, and they walk around holding claws—"

"Lobsters do not mate for life," I argued. "Female lobsters take turns with the dominant male in a given area."

"Huh. That's a very different type of relationship than the one I'd imagined," he said, his brow wrinkling. "That pokes some holes in my theory."

"Setting aside biology for a minute, I do believe it," I said. "Everyone has a lobster, but you have to haul up a lot of empty traps before you find it."

"Isn't that half the fun?" Cole asked with a smirk.

"If you had to estimate," I started, reaching for my beer, "how many broken hearts did you leave back in California?"

Cole rocked back with laughter. "I don't need to estimate," he said. "It's zero."

"Oh, great. You're one of those assholes who doesn't even realize he's beaten the shit out of someone's heart," I replied. "That doesn't bode well for me."

"I am not one of *those* assholes," he said, still laughing. "I'm an entirely different breed of asshole. The kind who works too much and never has time for relationships. After a while, not having time for relationships turns into forgetting how to be in relationships. Then that turns into forgetting how to speak to people who don't work for you. Not long after reaching that point, your virginity grows back and you start researching the monastic approach to life."

"Or sailing to Maine?" I asked.

"Well, yes," Cole replied with hesitance. "But I took to the water because I needed time away from my business. Things weren't going well. No, that's not accurate. The business is strong, really strong—"

"I've seen your boat, babe," I replied, my tone right on the edge of salty and surly. "You also offered me thirty grand to stay in my nine-by-nine guest room. You don't have to pull out your earnings statement."

"All fair points." He nodded to himself before continuing, "But now you have me wondering. How many broken hearts do you have to your name?"

"I don't do hearts," I lied. "My history is of the no-strings variety."

Cole stared at me for a long beat, his gaze inscrutable. "I'm not sure I believe that," he said. "You bring fish to nursing homes. You drive yourself crazy with budgets and regulatory guidance for the town council. You ask after Fitzy's son when everyone else avoids the topic. You marry the innkeepers because they don't have any family. You take in lost sailors even when they fuck up your nights." He shook his head. "You're all heart, Bartlett. All strings."

"Maybe," I conceded. "But I haven't broken anyone's heart. I'm certain of it."

"Not yet," Cole replied. "You seem like the kind of guy who would have a dog. You're the grumpiest motherfucker I've ever met but that crusty shell only hides a sweet, gooey center. Like crème brûlée. So, tell me. Why don't you have a dog?"

"I did," I said softly, glancing down with an aching sigh. "I did, and she was the best dog in the world. Sheilagh. She was the best girl."

"Oh," he murmured. "Oh, shit. I'm sorry. I shouldn't have brought it up."

"It's okay." I shook my head and looked away. "She lived a long life, and she really was the best girl. Before the arthritis took her legs, she loved coming on the boat with me every day. She loved the water. She'd run up and down the deck, barking at the seagulls. I knew...I knew when it was time. I just didn't have the strength to put her down."

"I'm sure." Cole reached across the table and took my hand. "That must have been a difficult time."

I shrugged. "She loved catching rays at the lighthouse. She'd lie down in front every afternoon, when the sun was right overhead."

He regarded me for several moments, his hand warm over mine and his eyes crinkled with concern. "It's a nice spot," he said.

"I left her at the house when I went out on the water one day," I continued, "and when I got home, I couldn't find her. Then I knew. I knew she went to the lighthouse, and—and she was gone." I gulped down a knot of emotion. "She didn't want to be a bother to anyone. She wanted to nestle into her favorite spot on a sunny day and close her eyes."

Cole's hand retreated, and he scooted out of his side of the booth. He came around the table, settled beside me, and brought his arm around my shoulders. "Owen," he whispered. "I'm so sorry."

"I buried her there, at the lighthouse. On the side with all the beach plum bushes." I ran my free hand down my face. "Cried the whole damn time," I admitted with a laugh.

"Have you thought about adopting another dog?" he asked. "Not that you can replace Sheilagh."

"I have thought about it." I jerked my shoulders. "But whenever I think about it, the time isn't right. Puppies are a lot of work, and I—I don't know that I can do it."

"You need a dog," Cole said. "And I need to stop with the depressing questions."

We sat there for several minutes, Cole's arm tight around my torso and his lips pressed to my temple. It was then I noticed the quiet in the tavern. Glancing up, I found the citizens of Talbott's Cove watching us. JJ was frozen behind the bar, a rag in one hand, a dripping glass in the other. A group of waiters were clustered nearby, their arms crossed over their chests. Patrons sat motionless, their forks still and eyes wide. Even Annette stopped reading long enough to glance in our direction.

"We have an audience," I whispered to Cole.

I felt him smile. "I know."

JJ shook free from his stare and set down his towel and glass. "There's nothin' to see here," he shouted, his Down East accent thicker than ever. "Eat ya food, mind ya business. All of you now. If ya want to gawk at my customers, get the hell outta here."

A gust of relief blew through me. I'd never expected anything short of acceptance from these people, but the world was packed with contradiction. Good people often made hateful choices. Friends turned their backs and families closed their doors. It mattered that JJ was willing to speak up for us, more than I'd expected.

I cupped Cole's face and kissed him. It was quick—as quick as I could be with him—and when I pulled back, life in The Galley was back to normal. "Thanks for coming over here," I said. "I like having you next to me."

His eyebrows arched up. "You like easy access to my dick."

"I enjoy both of those things," I said, laughing as I dropped my hand to his thigh. "I'll think about it. A dog. I need some time."

Cole shook his head. "I know how you are," he said. "You need to think everything through."

"You should know Sheilagh used to sleep on the bed with me," I said. "If she was still alive, she would've climbed on top of you and slept there."

"Cozy," he murmured. "Hey. That's interesting." He jerked his chin toward the far end of the bar. I craned my neck to see a man at Annette's side. "Who's that?"

"Jackson Lau," I said. We were flat-out staring now,

and we weren't the only ones. All the eyes that had once been on us were now trained on them. Talbott's Cove operated an equal opportunity gossip mill. "The town's chief of police."

Jackson pulled his wallet from his back pocket, thumbed out some cash, and dropped it on the bar. He brought his hand to her lower back and tipped his head toward the exit.

"It looks like they're...friendly," Cole said. "And by 'friendly' I mean he's fucked—"

"*No*." I speared him with a sharp glare. "This is one situation where I don't want your filthy thoughts."

With her lips pursed, Annette hopped off the barstool and shoved her book into a tote bag. She went to sling it over her shoulder but Jackson relieved her of it first. She scowled at him. I couldn't explain the genesis of this feeling, but I was proud of her. I wanted to high-five her, and tell her to make him work for it.

"Yeah, they're very *friendly*," I said.

"See? It was a good thing that you broke up with her," he said.

I rolled my eyes. "I didn't break up with her."

"Close enough," he replied.

Jackson and Annette crossed the restaurant, his hand low on her back and a town's-worth of eyes following them. She glanced in our direction as they passed, and offered a small smile.

"That is interesting," I said under my breath, waving to her in response.

"I'm just glad she's found her own man and stopped pining over mine," Cole said.

I swiveled away from Annette and Jackson to face Cole. "What?" I asked.

He lifted his beer to his lips, smiling. "You heard me," he replied. "You know I'd bite your neck and piss a circle around you, too."

My heart slammed into my throat so hard I was certain I'd choke on it. "Yeah," I said. Then, quietly, "It's nice to hear you say it, little prince."

twenty-one
COLE

All Night In: *v. Having no night watches.*

TONIGHT WAS similar to the last time we walked through the woods under the close-aired darkness. Similar yet loaded with difference. We walked hand-in-hand now, not rebelling against our connection but accepting it, cultivating it, sharing it. We didn't need alcohol to loosen our lips and embolden our actions. We knew the path would lead us home, and from there, it would take us to bed—together. It was good, and this was right.

We stumbled down the path—not as a result of liquor, though it had some hand in this—clinging to each other as we broke out in fits of riotous laughter. "I couldn't tell whether JJ was going to hop over the bar and drag us out by the scruff or launch into a slow clap," I said.

"Such an odd moment," Owen said with a chuckle.

"Did you see the look Brooke-Ashley gave him? She rolled her eyes so hard they still haven't come back around."

"True story," I murmured. "It was nice of the O'Keefes to drop by and say hello, even if they were a little awkward about it."

"Yeah, they're kind people," Owen replied. "They've had a few tough years, and they've struggled, but they'd still give you their last slice of bread if you asked for it."

I still didn't understand this town or the people in it, but neither were a puzzle in need of solving.

Owen turned, pinning me with a fierce stare. "But I don't want to talk about them anymore," he said.

"Okay," I replied. "That's fine. Maybe you can compliment my ass some more. That's what you're supposed to do on a date."

"I don't want to play pretend anymore," he said, his words quick and sharp. "I want to be real with you now."

"We are real," I said, confused. "Of course we're real. This entire night has been real. We weren't pretending to be on a date, Owen. We actually were on a—"

"I don't want you to go," he interrupted, "when the summer ends."

Boom. Just fucking *boom* went my heart.

"Say something." He stepped closer, pressing his chest to mine. If his declaration wasn't enough to stun me into silence, his cock, hardening under his shorts, did the trick. "Tell me what you're thinking."

"I—*ohhh*—yeah," I stammered, widening my stance and arching toward the firm ridge of him. He rocked against me, grinning as I groaned. "I can't think when you do that, baby."

"Try, for me, baby. Try. Promise me you'll stay." Owen's hips were bucking against me in a lazy rhythm. We groaned at that, and I was ready to come all over us. It could have been the friction, but it was mostly his words. "Say something," he repeated, the order taking on an edge of anxiety.

"Yes, I want you," I replied with a needy groan. The dry friction of his clothing-covered dick rubbing against mine made it impossible to do anything other than sink into these sensations. "Of course."

"That's right," he said, growling.

"I want to stay," I continued, the loose tooth of my life outside this town wiggling under these words. "I want to stay here with *you*. But I should tell you—"

"The only thing you have to tell me is how you want me fucking you," he said as he pushed me against a tree.

A gasp burst from my lips as the trunk bit into my back. With a shaking hand, I reached for Owen's jaw. I canted his face up, wanting to see the wild in his eyes. "Not this time," I whispered.

My hand still gripping his face, I stepped away from the tree. I curled my fingers around his belt and jerked his hips flush with mine. I wanted him like nothing else. So much that it hurt. But I also wanted this—him, us, these woods—and I couldn't bring myself to stop.

"What do you think you're doing, McClish?" he asked.

My eyes drifted shut while I basked in the pleasure of his shaft rubbing against mine. Even through layers of clothing, the sensation was unreal. "Could I make you come?" I asked. "Just like this?"

Owen's hand shifted from my waist to my backside. He held me, squeezing just a bit. "You could smile at me, and I'd fall apart," he whispered. His fingers skimmed down my ass, pressing and rubbing like a dream. "I think you know that."

"I don't," I said, my voice tight as I held back a groan. With all the strength I could gather, I positioned him against the tree, pecked a kiss on the corner of his mouth, and dropped to my knees. "My turn."

This time, I handled both his button and zipper without incident, and yanked his boxer briefs down. He loved it when I played with him a bit, teased, but I'd do all that some other time. Tonight, I was hungry for him. Hungry for a piece to call my own.

Owen's hand skimmed up the back of my neck. "Baby, no. You don't have to."

"I want to," I said, my eyes trained on his thick shaft. With his thighs trembling and flexing under my hands, I dragged my tongue up his cock. He was hot and delicious, and I wasted no time taking him in my mouth.

"Goddamn," Owen hissed.

I pushed a finger inside him, just past the rim, and he howled. Actually fucking *howled*. His hips jerked away from the tree trunk, thrusting into my mouth. His hands were in my hair and his thigh was stiff under my free hand. He was leaking and twitching in small, quick pulses. Just like waves at low tide.

I kissed down his length and across his sac. "Good?" I asked, glancing up at him.

"Would it be cliché to tell you I love you right now?" he asked. "Because I do. I really fucking do."

My world lit up then, a riot of heat and joy, and a fullness, like being swaddled in a tight embrace. The words were burning on my tongue, but I couldn't offer them in return until I was certain he meant them. Owen wasn't one for hyperbole but I had to be sure.

"No clichés," I replied, smiling against his thigh. "My blowjobs are *that* good."

"Get up here," Owen ordered, hooking his hands under my arms and urging me off the ground.

When I pushed to my feet, he took my face in his hands and kissed me hard. He nipped at my tongue, bit my lip, and I bit right back. His pants were still tangled around his ankles, and I stole this opportunity to slide my fingers along his seam.

"I want to fuck you right here but I don't think tree sap makes for the best lube," I said.

I felt Owen smile against my neck. "Let's not do that," he said. "The tree sap lube, that is. I quite enjoy natural products, but that's over the line for me. The rest of it sounds great."

I rubbed my free hand up and down his chest, pawing at him. "You want me to fuck you?"

"The answer to that question has always been yes," he said. "Always will be."

After another biting kiss, I turned him around in my arms. My hips rolled against his backside, my cock right between his cheeks while I stroked him. I was cross-eyed and crazy with lust, and *this close* to spitting into my palm and fucking him raw.

Rarely did I feel the desire to take a man like this, but with Owen, I had a desperate, panting need that I felt rising up from deep within me. I wanted to have him, be *with* him in every place possible way, brand him as my own.

"That settles it," I said. "I'm taking my man home now."

twenty-two
OWEN

Outward Bound: *adj. Leaving the safety of port, heading out to open ocean.*

THIS WAS *THE* NIGHT.

The one when I came out—all the way out—to the town.

The one when we made a tradition out of blowjobs in the woods.

The one when I confessed my love for Cole and didn't have a nervous breakdown when he laughed off my words.

And also the one when Cole led me into the bedroom, stripped me naked, and guided me to the bed so he could tease me with his tongue for approximately nine years while I dissolved into a bright, shimmering disaster of love and need and hope. Now, I was gasping and quivering, on the verge of goddamn tears as he pushed inside me. It wasn't pain that dampened my eyes but an ache, a spasm far inside me that only grew as I watched his cock sliding into my body. I loved this man, I loved him more than I understood.

"How's that?" Cole asked, shifting his hips a bit as he inched in. His eyes were hooded, his teeth pressed into his lower lip, his breath coming in shallow pants. "Tell me it's good because you feel amazing."

"Good, good," I said, gasping as he stretched me. My cock was weeping all over my belly but I couldn't focus on anything but the glorious pressure between my legs. "Keep going. You're doing great, baby. You're perfect."

He stared at me, smiling like he knew a secret, and I was absolutely helpless. But I was the one with the secret. My sweet, silly man with his clumsiness and his arrogant streak. He was everything to me, and I was dying to be everything to him.

Cole ran his hand up the back of my thigh, pushing it closer to my chest as he seated himself. He closed his eyes and dropped his head back. For a moment, neither of us moved. He blew out a breath and gripped my thighs hard, as if he needed an anchor to hold himself back. I didn't want that.

"Come here," I whispered, beckoning him closer. His dick was inside me and somehow, he was too far away.

Cole nodded and positioned my legs around his waist. "Oh, fuck," he murmured, his eyes rolling back as he found a rhythm. "I mean it. You're amazing. I'm never bottoming again."

"That's not an option," I said. I reached for him, first grabbing his flanks, then his shoulders, and finally lashing my arms around his torso when we were chest-to-chest.

My lips found his neck, and I breathed a content sigh because I had him. Inside me, around me, everywhere. "I love fucking your ass. You're not taking that away from me."

"And I love *you*," he started, "so I won't."

A laugh burst from my lips, unbidden. He was thrusting into me now, slow and hard, but that pleasure was a distant second to the one seizing my heart.

"You made me wait," I said, smiling up at him. "You walked me home, licked my ass for half-a-fucking-hour, and waited until you were balls deep inside me to say that." I arched up to meet his lips, hoping my kiss would tell him how much he pushed me, and how much I needed those pushes. "I love you."

Cole grinned, nodding. "I know," he said, reaching between us to wrap his fingers around my cock. "Would it be cliché of me to come right now? Because I'm damn close."

I shook my head, the words tangled up in a knot of emotion heavy in my chest. I *loved* this man, and he...he loved me, too. Those words weren't ones I'd heard before, it wasn't a feeling anyone had reciprocated.

The fast slide of his hand over my length kept me on the edge but it was the blissful sighs stuttering past his lips as he slammed into me that did it. That pushed me over, broke me apart, and patiently sewed me back together again.

Tonight was *the* night but that didn't mean it was the only night. This could only get better.

twenty-three
OWEN

Rogue Wave: n. *A large, unexpected and suddenly appearing surface wave that can be extremely dangerous.*

IT WAS LATE SEPTEMBER, and I was in Portland for the monthly meeting of the Maine Lobster Conservancy's board of directors. It was true what they said about the squeaky wheels getting the grease, except this squeaky wheel had been nominated for a board seat after complaining about the issues long enough. I still preferred the ocean to the office but it was rewarding to know that I was making some small difference.

But this meeting couldn't adjourn quickly enough. Tomorrow marked the eight-week anniversary of Cole's arrival in Talbott's Cove, and we were starting the celebration with a special dinner tonight.

These weeks had been nothing short of magical, and I wasn't the kind of guy who threw words like those around. With Cole, I felt things I'd never before experienced. I wanted things, too. Things I'd never thought available to me.

Love. Family. Forever. And I really wanted it all with him.

So I was laying it all out there tonight. I was loading him up with the best steaks and wine I could find, and I was telling him that I wanted to make this official. It was time for him to move in, all the way. We could convert one of the extra bedrooms to a proper office. He could get rid of his place in California. Obviously, he could run his business from Maine. He'd managed just fine for almost two months.

He'd move in, we'd fix up an office, and we'd have a life together. And maybe...maybe we could plan a trip down to Cape Cod next summer to exchange vows. A visit to P-Town would do him good.

That *maybe* had my heart plotting an escape from my chest because *maybe* had to be *yes*. Had to be.

Cole was in charge of dessert tonight. I was hoping that consisted of nothing more than a dollop of whipped cream on my fiancé's dick.

Repairs finished on Cole's boat early last week, but that event came and went with little fanfare. It was an amazing craft—now that it wasn't on the fritz and running aground—and we took it for a sail down to the Isle of Shoals over the weekend. It was a nice break from our usual routine, one we needed. Life was great, but it was busy. The lobster season was hitting its peak, and Cole was spending more time on work projects when we weren't hauling in traps.

Even though it meant a decrease in our time together, I

understood that Cole needed to work. That he'd been able to spend the summer working my decks was a gift, one I knew wouldn't last forever. He had a conference call a few days ago, and though I didn't mean to eavesdrop on the entire thing, I found myself addicted to his authoritative tone. It didn't matter what he was saying. I liked in-charge Cole. I wanted more of him.

Instead of staying to talk shop after the meeting, I hustled out and headed to downtown Portland. My grocery list was long, and I had exactly seven minutes to find everything I needed and get on the road if we were going to eat before Thursday Night Football kicked off. It was situations like these that made me reconsider Cole's desire to install one of those DVR things.

He was gentle like that, always nudging me to try new things but never forcing. He didn't care that I hated bourbon or reading books on electronic screens, or that I preferred the butt plug in *his* ass. I wasn't as gentle. The solitary life I'd once considered adequate was now filled with affection and laughter, but that hadn't beaten the cranky bastard out of me.

Perhaps that was why I was sighing like a moody teenager and drumming my fingers on the grocery cart while the woman ahead of me handed the cashier a wad of coupons thicker than the Bible. Food, our future, football, fucking. That was the plan for tonight, and Coupon Cathy was screwing up my schedule with her thriftiness.

Craning my neck to find a quicker line, I found myself staring at the last person I expected to find in Portland: Cole. Except it wasn't him, not the Cole *I* knew. It was a polished-up, slick-haired, fake-smile, suit-and-tie version of him with "Where In The World Is Cole McClish?" printed across his chest.

Why is my man *on the cover of a magazine and why the fuck are people wondering where he is?*

I snatched the magazine from the rack and flipped to the article about Cole while I steered my cart to the short order line. I didn't care whether I had many more than ten items. If the cashier noticed, she didn't care either. Maybe I was the one who didn't notice as the only thought in my head was an infinite loop of *I thought I knew him* while I read.

Paying, leaving the store, getting into my truck, driving home—I remembered none of it. I did, however, remember every word of that cover story about Cole. I couldn't handle this. I'd given this man everything, all of me, and I'd thought I was getting all of him in return.

But there was always more to Cole's story. Secrets, histories, situations I didn't understand and couldn't bring myself to explore. But I'd convinced myself reality wasn't too far divorced from the fantasy. He was wealthy and accomplished, and held enough sway to take the summer off without issue. I could handle that. His reality was a slim fraction of the one I'd imagined, one that foreclosed all possibility of a future for us.

There was no place for me in a world that involved epic fortunes.

I was a tough guy, a strong guy. Being a lobsterman did that to me, and being alone for all these years did it, too. I didn't consider myself sensitive or delicate, but everything about this fucking hurt. Throughout the ride back to Talbott's Cove, I kept a fist pressed to my chest to hold back the rising ache.

He was on the couch when I arrived, his long legs stretched out, computer on his lap, glasses perched on his head. I was all out of words, and couldn't offer more than a slammed door in greeting.

"Hey, what's..." His voice trailed off when I turned the magazine toward him. "Oh, *shit*."

"That's it?" I barked. "All you've got for me is *oh, shit*? You're a fucking billionaire and you've invented, like, the *entire internet*, and you never thought any of that was worth mentioning? You didn't think I deserved a heads-up on that one?"

Cole closed his computer and stared at the floor. Seconds that felt a whole fuckton like hours passed without a word.

"I'm sorry." He stood, wincing at the magazine as he approached me. "I didn't mean for it to happen like"—he glanced at the magazine that hung from my hand like an old-timey wanted poster—"that. But you said you didn't want to know. I tried to tell you."

Somewhere along the way, I'd stopped thinking of him as a fantasy. I allowed myself to forget the corners of his life he kept from me, and in that forgetfulness, I believed he could be mine.

Never once had I braced myself for the kind of status and acclaim that would put his face on magazines. It wasn't a matter of our worlds being different anymore.

"There's a difference between knowing you're wealthy

and important, and *this*." I shook the magazine at him. It didn't matter that I'd asked him to spare me the details of his life on the West Coast. That I asked for the lies. "I know my world is nothing like yours. I've always known that. I had no idea you're the master of the online universe. You're fuckin' internet royalty."

"That's an exaggeration." Frowning, he folded his arms over his chest. "I'm not internet royalty."

"The fuck you aren't," I cried.

"Royalty suggests power by bloodline." He shrugged. "I wasn't born into this. I'm more of an alchemist."

"Oh, my God, Cole," I shouted. "Shut the hell up."

He was decent enough to stop talking and hold up his hands in surrender.

"The article said you were in search of a 'creative lightning rod' and a 'spiritual, strategic reawakening,' whatever the fuck that means. What was this to you?" I asked. "Some kind of experiment? Head up to Maine, fuck a lobsterman, and find your next great idea?"

"Of course not," he said. "I was wrong. I should've told you, and I wanted to tell you so many times."

"But you decided to keep right on hiding instead," I roared. "You're good at that, aren't you? You ran away from Silicon Valley after some app that didn't work. That's why you're here, right?"

"None of that matters, Owen," he argued. "You're the only one who knows me, the real me. You have to believe me."

I turned away from him, shifting my gaze to the ocean.

"I thought I knew you, but that article makes it clear that I don't."

"I can tell you right now that article is bullshit. There are news stories and blog posts written about me every day. Entire books about me, my company, my approach to business. I know this is all new to you, but—"

"I'm not stupid, Cole," I interrupted.

He brought his fingertips to his forehead and rubbed his temples. "That's not what I was saying. I was wrong, Owen. I should've told you. Held you down and forced you to listen. But I loved that you knew me, the guy who drifted into the Cove, not the internet royalty." His lips quirked up in a rueful smile. "You found me and you took me in when I was lost and lonely. You accepted the guy who fell overboard. The one who required a lesson on dishwashing and pestered you with a thousand questions. I wanted you to love *that* guy, and not the one with an industry on his shoulders."

"I *did* love that guy, but I can't love this guy," I said, gesturing to the magazine.

"Goddamn it, Owen," he yelled. "Don't say that. Don't fucking say that."

Summer love was never meant for me. It wasn't mine to keep. I built sandcastle dreams and the tides washed them away every time.

"I think you should go."

Cole's eyes drifted shut, his head fell forward, and his shoulders slumped. For an instant, my heart ached to comfort him. And goddamn him for that. Even at my most gutted, I still wanted to care for him.

These four walls were soaked with memories of these past eight weeks—of *us*—and I couldn't drown in them, not now. I dropped the magazine and marched to the porch. The sea would soothe me tonight.

"Don't be here when I get back."

twenty-four
COLE

Cut and Run: *v. The fast but expensive practice of sailing away quickly, either by cutting free an anchor or by cutting ropeyarns to unfurl sails from the yards.*

Cole: Did you know about TechToday's cover story?
Neera: I did not. They didn't reach out to me or the communications shop for comment.
Cole: But you knew it was released? And didn't think I needed to know that?
Neera: Yes, I knew it was released.
Neera: No, I didn't think it was worth notifying you. It was unremarkable. Dozens of similar stories have been printed in recent weeks.
Neera: Is there an issue?
Cole: Issues, plural.
Neera: Understood. How can I help?

Cole: I'm going to need your assistance.

Cole: Get my replacement on the phone.

Neera: I'll take care of it.

Cole: Get a pilot and a jet ready. If the next day doesn't shake out the way I'm hoping it will, I'm going to need a ride home.

Neera: May I ask what's happening in the next day?

Cole: I'm begging the love of my life to take me back despite my extremely long list of flaws, inadequacies, and missteps.

Neera: Very well. Where might this jet be picking you up?

Cole: I'm in Talbott's Cove, Maine.

Neera: Forgive me for asking but if things do go as you're hoping, do you anticipate staying there?

Cole: I'd like to. If he lets me.

Neera: Then I'll do whatever I can to make that happen.

Cole: Thank you. I appreciate it, N.

Neera: That's what I'm here for.

Neera: I figured you'd find one spot and stay there for the summer. I'm happy you found that spot, and someone to share it with.

Cole: What?

Neera: The bookstore you asked me to feature is in Talbott's Cove. And the oceanic nonprofits you asked me to signal boost are also in Maine.

Neera: I also received an invoice from the sailboat fabricators last week. It referenced delivering parts to Talbott's Cove Marina.

Cole: You knew? All this time, you knew where I was and you didn't come find me?

Neera: You didn't want me to find you.
Neera: I believe you were busy finding yourself.

THERE WERE benefits to being a billionaire. I didn't worry about having a roof over my head or food on the table. The health and well-being of my parents, sisters, and nieces and nephews was secure.

And whenever I needed to make a call without the benefit of mobile service, I had a satellite at the ready.

With a secure connection in place, I explained my issues with that *TechToday* click-bait bullshit to my acting CEO and PR team. There was none of my usual Scream, Fire, or Throw. Not when I was fighting to keep the tears out of my voice.

Apparently, the newer, calmer Cole was absolutely terrifying because they were snapping to attention and suggesting every countermeasure imaginable, short of putting a hit on the journalist. The acting CEO was even amenable to my proposals, and that right there was progress.

For all that I could solve with money, there were several things I couldn't. One of them—my grumpy, growly bear—was somewhere in Jericho Bay by now. Knowing Owen, he'd sooner tuck his big body into the *Sweet Carolyne*'s cramped quarters and spend an uncomfortable night at sea than risk seeing me again.

He wasn't wrong. I hadn't shown myself worthy of his presence, not when I'd let months pass without telling him everything. There were opportunities to put it all on the table, and I should've ignored his request to the contrary. I pushed him to be honest and real with Annette, even when staying hidden was the easiest route. I should've taken some of my own advice. Instead, I usually seized those opportunities to suck his dick or get bent over the kitchen table. I always wanted him wrapped around me, and I knew talk of my other life wouldn't give me that. I knew it would come between us because it came between me and everything.

But that didn't mean I was accepting it, not this time. Not with Owen.

I sat on the dock for hours, long after the sun had slipped past the horizon. The lighthouse blinked out a golden beam, a silent reminder that I wasn't alone in watching over the water. My ass was sore and my heart was heavy, but I was staying right there until Owen returned.

When the boat's light cut through the darkness, an hour or two before dawn, I found him staring at me, his gaze hard and hurt.

"I told you to leave," he yelled from the deck. He turned away, busying himself with lines and buoys.

"That's tough shit, Owen," I called as he stepped onto the dock. "We need to talk."

He froze, his fists on his hips and his head hanging low. "Please," he said, his voice strained. "I can't do this."

I wrapped my hand around his bicep and pulled him close. "I fucked up and I was wrong but I love you, and you can't just toss me back into the sea."

Sighing, Owen looked out at the dark waters of the cove. "Your life...it's not here."

One of his greatest powers was his stoicism. He could hear my most sacred, private words and respond with little more than an impatient exhale. A blink. But I knew him, and I knew there was more to him than that. He wanted to be loved as much as I did, and he wanted me to keep pushing. His walls might be tall, but I wasn't afraid of the climb.

"It can be," I said.

That caught his attention, but holy Jesus, I wanted to hold him tight when he gave me that sad, pouty bear face.

"I mean that. I can stay. My life can be anything I want it to be. Anything we want."

His eyebrow winged up, unconvinced. "It seems that you're needed back in Silicon Valley."

"I'm not going back to the Valley, at least not permanently. I kinda hate it there." I shrugged, and he continued watching me with *what are you talking about?* eyes. "They'll be fine without me, and I can build apps to make working remotely more seamless." I dropped my hands to my waist, my hip cocked. "There's also the issue of my boyfriend living in Maine, and long distance just won't work for us."

"Then...what are you going to do?" he asked.

I brought my palm to the back of his neck. "Being here helped me realize that I didn't like managing the business. I'd always known, but...it was the only thing I had, you know? Now I know I'd rather mess around with crazy ideas and fix wonky code issues, and none of that requires me to spend any time in the office. I can do it anywhere, as long as I'm with you."

Owen didn't say anything for a long, painful minute where I was more interested in drowning myself than having him turn me away again. But finally—*fucking finally*—he wrapped his arm around my waist and dropped his head to my shoulder. "This probably means you're going to want that Wi-Fi stuff in the house now, huh?"

I laughed and rubbed my hand down his back. "I installed it in July," I said.

He lifted a shoulder but didn't respond immediately. "I let myself think this would work out, you know, with us. That I could ignore your life before me, and we could live in this little bubble. Then I saw that magazine, and..." He sighed, and that warm puff set off a ripple of goose bumps over my neck. "And I felt like a fool. That's why I wanted you to leave. Not because I didn't want you."

His words were the sharpest arrows.

"I mean it, Owen. I'm so sorry. Tell me how I can make it up to you."

"No more secrets," he murmured. "And you could say yes when I ask you to marry me."

"Yes," I said. "Yes now, and yes always."

epilogue
OWEN

Reef Knot: n. Joining two ends of a single line to bind around an object.

FIFTEEN MONTHS *later*

"WHAT IS THIS UNHOLY MESS?" I asked from the doorway as I shook out of my sleet-soaked coat. A nor'easter was blowing in tonight.

Cole glanced up at me but quickly returned to the measuring cups and mixing bowls on the countertop. "I thought you'd be out for another two hours," he replied.

"You didn't answer my question," I said.

"You didn't stick to your schedule," he answered, pushing his glasses up his nose. His fingers were dusted with flour, leaving a white smudge on his dark frames.

Once I'd shucked off my cold, wet outerwear, I padded into the kitchen to get a look at the chaos brewing there.

"It smells good," I remarked, glancing at the sheet trays cooling near the oven. "Whatever it is."

"I made gingerbread," Cole said as he poured sugar into a mixing bowl.

I took another look around the kitchen. "For the entire town?"

"For a gingerbread house," he replied. "I'm constructing a scale replica of the house. And the lighthouse." He tapped the measuring cup against the bowl before turning on the mixer, the shine of his wedding band catching my eye. I couldn't fight the grin that surfaced every time I noticed it on his finger, or the obscenely sweet photo of our first dance that was framed and hung above the fireplace. "I'm making frosting now."

We were a few days away from our six month anniversary. We'd intended for our wedding to be a small affair, but I discovered my definition of "small" deviated from Cole's by fifty percent. In the end, it was a bit larger and more lavish than I would've selected for myself but getting married wasn't about me alone. If there was one thing I'd learned since Cole drifted into my life, it was that *we* mattered more than *I*.

"Um," I started, running my hands through my hair, "if you needed something to do, you could've helped me haul in traps. Were you bored or something?"

Cole still accompanied me on the boat most mornings, but not all the time. There were days and nights when he was too deep in his work to look up, and I respected the ebb and flow of his mind's machinations. When I left this morning, he appeared lost in his coding. No cakes in sight.

"I was working and now I'm baking," Cole answered over the whirring mixer. "It's the holidays, and I wanted to do something festive. Since we spent last year in Palm Springs with my mother—"

"Where we did *not* dehydrate into jerky," I said.

He glared at me over the mixer. "Since we spent last year in Palm Springs," he continued, "I wanted to start a tradition of our own this year."

"You were bored," I murmured.

Cole was between projects, and having that kind of time on his hands often led to him falling down curious rabbit holes. He tried his hand at gardening last summer. It yielded a handful of tomatoes and one amusingly girthy zucchini before he abandoned it to start building a new app. That product met with massive success.

The Talbott's Cove Effect. That's what Cole called it. Everything he created here was a hit.

As much as he loved being here, there were still moments when it was difficult for him to cede control to the people back in California. Those moments occurred only when he was locked in a power struggle over issues and details I didn't understand. Reliably, Neera talked him off those ledges.

She visited us in the Cove every month or so. She'd fly in for a weekend, and she and Cole would spend two hours working at the kitchen table. Then the three of us would hit the water. For reasons I still didn't understand, the lady enjoyed sorting lobsters. She was good at it, too. It only took a quick overview of the process and she sorted more quickly—and more accurately—than her boss.

Cole traveled to Silicon Valley from time to time, but he spent the majority of his time here in Maine. We'd flown out there—on a goddamn private jet, no less—a few months after everything hit the fan with his so-called disappearance last year. His company was introducing a new product, the one he'd developed while working as my deckhand, and he wanted me to join him for the launch party.

Before we'd arrived, I wanted to hate everything about California and his world there. It was fucked up, it was immature, it was irrational. The good news was that it didn't last.

Cole's house was big, modern, and boring, and I fucked him on just about every surface I could find. That seemed like the right way for him to say goodbye to that era of his life. Since he only visited California a few times each year now, he ditched the gigantic mansion and downsized into a penthouse apartment. If anyone could call a penthouse downsizing.

Palo Alto was different from Talbott's Cove for sure, but it was amazing. It was fast-paced and overflowing with people, and I loved it. I loved the vibe, the places, the weather, even the people who wore sneakers with business suits.

I'd worried I'd be intimidated by the people from his company, or they'd resent me for keeping him on the East Coast. None of that happened. They were fun and fascinating, and interested in hearing about our life in the Cove. One weird dude asked me about bringing a group out on the water for some lobster boat team building, and Cole damn near pissed himself laughing about that. Later, he told me I could indulge the offer, yell at some executives all morning, and charge six figures for my time.

I wasn't ashamed to say I gave it serious consideration.

If Talbott's Cove hadn't been inundated with wealthy businesspeople—and their tourism money—I would've gone along with that ridiculousness. But ever since Cole announced he'd be staying in Maine, the tech types had been flocking here. My sleepy seaside town was becoming the next Sun Valley.

The local inn was always booked, and some of the locals had taken to fixing up their homes and listing them on short-term rental websites for obscene rates. The O'Keefes were able to pay their daughter's college tuition after renting out their house for the summer *and* pay off their mortgage. JJ sprung for a new can of paint and added some kale salads to The Galley's menu. No one ordered them but it was an amusing gesture. The town council was slammed with proposals for restaurants, shops, hotels. It was madness.

The Cole McClish Effect. That's what I called it. Everyone wanted to catch some of the magic he found here.

"Yes, I hit a wall with my work but I also wanted to surprise you with a new tradition," Cole started, pinning me with a sharp glance, "but it seems you chose this as the one and only day you'll deviate from your schedule."

"The fish weren't biting," I said, laughing. "That's often the case when winter storms move in."

He looked up, his lips parting, and stared out at the

sleet and dark clouds. The visibility was low and the waves high. Based on the surprise washing over his face, he hadn't noticed until now. Absentmindedness was one of Cole's most adorable—but also infuriating—traits. I was certain the earth could open up and swallow everything around him, and he wouldn't notice until his ass caught on fire.

"You went out in that weather?" he asked, incredulous.

"Yes, sweetheart, I did." I pointed to my dripping hair. "That's why I'm soaked. Unlike some people, I don't make a habit of falling overboard."

"I haven't fallen over in"—Cole turned his gaze to the ceiling while he murmured to himself—"three or four months."

"It's almost a record," I replied.

Rolling his eyes, Cole scraped the sides of his mixing bowl with a spatula. "You didn't have to go out," he said. "You know I don't like it when you're on the water in bad weather."

It was my turn to roll my eyes. "You didn't notice the weather until now."

"That has no bearing on whether you should've been out there," Cole replied. "You could've looked outside, seen the storm, and gone back to bed. I would've joined you for that."

Lightening my fishing and lobstering load was one of Cole's side projects. To his mind, money wasn't an issue, and I didn't need to work the water every day. I agreed with him—to a point. Unlike years past, I wasn't compelled to go after other catches during lobster's slow season from January to June. I didn't sweat over expenses when the market prices dropped. But I wasn't interested in lightening the load any more than that. My objection was less about not wanting to be a kept man and more about enjoying my work. It was grueling but I still loved it, and I didn't want to abandon it.

Change wasn't easy and I didn't take to Cole's money overnight, but it wasn't a major point of contention for us. There were moments when I found his wealth staggering. Paralyzing, even. But I didn't want that to become a rock in the middle of our relationship. That took work. I had to practice dealing with the shock associated with spending loads of money as easily as he did. I rolled with it when Cole wanted to spend a month on a private island in Belize after the launch of one of his newest developments, and when he bought out an entire hotel in Palm Springs when we traveled there for the holidays last winter. Instead of getting caught up in the disparity between our income levels, I admired my husband's ass in short shorts.

"I had traps to pull in." I reached over, turned off the mixer, and held up a hand to silence Cole's protest. "Just be quiet for a minute. Please."

I glanced down at his apron, covered in floury handprints, and then back up at his face. There was a dark smudge on his cheek—probably molasses—and a bit of sugar sparkling on his brow. He was a beautiful mess, and I was the luckiest guy in the entire state.

"Don't look at me like that while I have gingerbread in the oven," Cole warned. "Save those bedroom eyes for later, babe."

I pressed my lips to his and sighed when his tongue darted out. He tugged me closer, until only our clothes separated us. "What about kitchen eyes?" I whispered against his jaw. "Can I have those?"

"What?" he asked, breathless as I dragged my denim-covered erection over his. "What are you talking about?"

I laughed, the tight sound bursting from my mouth in quick, strangled puffs. "I need to warm up, and you have one helluva hot ass. Do I have time to bend you over the countertop before the next cake comes out of the oven?" The words had barely passed my lips when the oven timer wailed. "*Fuck*."

Cole shook with silent laughter. "To answer your question, babe, no."

Before I could pry myself off him, I heard paws skittering down the hall. "Here comes trouble," I murmured.

Last winter, we rescued a three-year-old mixed breed dog from the local no-kill shelter. We waited until after the new year, when things settled down from Cole's big launch and we returned from our extended holiday in Palm Springs. I wasn't sure I was ready for another pup, but when we walked past Sasha's kennel, everything changed. Her sweet face and happy spirit stole our hearts.

"She snoozes until the timer goes off," Cole said. "Then she's my shadow. She's on crumb patrol."

"I don't doubt it." An eager, fidgeting mass of dog wedged between our legs, paws stamping and tail wagging. I reached down to scratch her head. "What's this? You'll wake up for gingerbread but not me?"

With a whine, she plopped down on her bottom, her

tail thumping against the hardwood. She was part Irish Setter, her coat a warm, glossy red, but the rest of her lineage was unclear. She had the temperament of a Labrador, the strength of a Boxer, and the lapdog sensibilities of a Maltese.

The oven timer pealed again, and Cole slipped out of my hold. "Since you won't be bending me over the countertop, you can help me with the gingerbread lighthouse," he said.

I crouched down to give Sasha some love. "What do you mean I'm not bending you over?" I asked.

"We're building this lighthouse, Owen," he warned. "We're going to have some traditions, and you're going to damn well enjoy them."

With a low groan, I pushed to my feet. Sasha nudged my leg with her nose, and I responded with another head scratch. She huffed and stalked toward Cole, more interested in sniffing out those crumbs than anything I had to offer. I stared at my husband from across the kitchen, smiling when he fed her a bit of gingerbread.

There was a time when I filled my life with quiet and order. When I'd accepted solitude as my only companion. But now my dog was begging for scratch-made baked goods. My man was inventing holiday traditions. My finger wore a shiny new ring. My home was full of noise, clutter, and chaos.

"I will, Cole," I said. "I promise I'll enjoy it all."

And my heart, it was overflowing with the kind of love I'd never imagined for myself.

THANK you for reading *Fresh Catch*! I hope you love Cole and Owen. If you enjoyed this visit to Talbott's Cove, you'll love Annette and Jackson in *Hard Pressed.*

Dear Jackson,

I'm leaving you this note because I know you're very busy and I don't want to waste the town sheriff's time. Lord knows I've already wasted enough of it.

Thank you for taking me home last night and…everything else. I made you a basket of wild blueberry muffins for your trouble. That seemed like the appropriate baked good for getting naked in your living room.

I wasn't myself last night. I didn't mean to kiss you or fondle your backside or ask all those intimate questions. Thank you for pretending to enjoy it.

It was very noble of you to sleep on the couch while I was starfished on your bed. I couldn't help but notice it's quite large. The bed, that is. I swear, I didn't notice anything else when I let myself out this morning.

As you know, Talbott's Cove is a ridiculously small town and there's no chance we can avoid each other. Not that I'd want to avoid you, of course, but I'm not sure I can look at you without thinking of the forty different ways I made a fool of myself.

Instead of avoidance, let's try to be friends. We'll forget all about last night…if that's what you want.

Please burn this note after you read it—

. . .

Annette

P.S. I whipped up some cinnamon buns, too. Please enjoy them. I'm not sure why, but I couldn't get buns out of my mind today.

HARD PRESSED **IS AVAILABLE NOW!**

Join Kate Canterbary's Office Memos mailing list for occasional news and updates, as well as new release alerts, exclusive extended epilogues and bonus scenes, and cake. There's always cake.

Visit Kate's private reader group to chat about books, get early peeks at new books, and hang out with over booklovers!

If newsletters aren't your jam, follow Kate on BookBub for preorder and new release alerts.

also by kate canterbary

Vital Signs

Before Girl — Cal and Stella

The Worst Guy — Sebastian Stremmel and Sara Shapiro

The Walsh Series

Underneath It All – Matt and Lauren

The Space Between – Patrick and Andy

Necessary Restorations – Sam and Tiel

The Cornerstone – Shannon and Will

Restored — Sam and Tiel

The Spire — Erin and Nick

Preservation — Riley and Alexandra

Thresholds — The Walsh Family

Foundations — Matt and Lauren

The Santillian Triplets

The Magnolia Chronicles — Magnolia

Boss in the Bedsheets — Ash and Zelda

The Belle and the Beard — Linden and Jasper-Anne

Talbott's Cove

Fresh Catch — Owen and Cole

Hard Pressed — Jackson and Annette

Far Cry — Brooke and JJ

Rough Sketch — Gus and Neera

Benchmarks Series

Professional Development — Drew and Tara

Orientation — Jory and Max

Brothers In Arms

Missing In Action — Wes and Tom

Coastal Elite — Jordan and April

Get exclusive sneak previews of upcoming releases through Kate's newsletter and private reader group, The Canterbary Tales, on Facebook.

about kate

USA Today Bestseller Kate Canterbary writes smart, steamy contemporary romances loaded with heat, heart, and happy ever afters. Kate lives on the New England coast with her husband and daughter.

You can find Kate at www.katecanterbary.com

- facebook.com/kcanterbary
- twitter.com/kcanterbary
- instagram.com/katecanterbary
- amazon.com/Kate-Canterbary
- bookbub.com/authors/kate-canterbary
- goodreads.com/Kate_Canterbary
- pinterest.com/katecanterbary
- tiktok.com/@katecanterbary

acknowledgments

I want to thank Jessica Fletcher for making me believe in small towns and craggy lobstermen, and my grandmother for introducing me to Mrs. Fletcher.

I'd also like to thank Lynn Faust, the leading expert on fireflies in the Smoky Mountain region.

Finally, my husband's support (and patience and tolerance for me typing in bed at two in the morning) is the most important ingredient in all of my books.

Printed in Great Britain
by Amazon